40¢

BRYHER – RUAN

★

*By the same author*

The Fourteenth of October

The Player's Boy

Roman Wall

Beowulf

Gate to the Sea

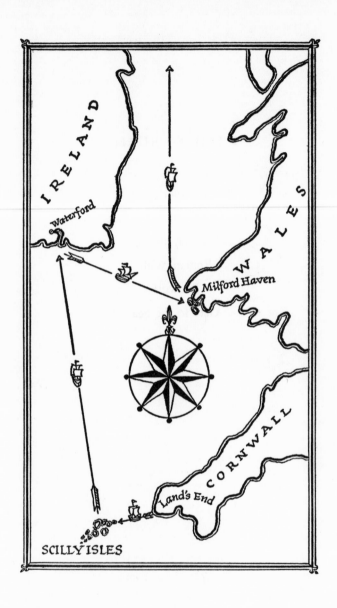

# RUAN

by Bryher

PANTHEON BOOKS
A Division of Random House
NEW YORK

*21,609*

FOR DORIS

*who took me to the islands*

# FOREWORD

E have learned a great deal recently about the early history of Britain, due both to new scientific techniques and to the amazing interest in archaeology that has sprung up in England since the last war. It takes about twenty years, however, before such fresh discoveries are included in school textbooks, and as sixth-century Britain is hardly a subject that will be familiar to many readers, it seems essential to give a brief account of the time. In all cases, dates are approximate and may vary by a few years.

The British under the leadership of Arthur are said to have defeated the Saxons decisively at Badon about A.D. 517. Later, a civil war occurred that ended with the

7

deaths of both Arthur and his opponent, Medraut, at the battle of Camlann about 538.

My story is set about a generation after this period. The Saxons were still quiet but Irish raiders were plundering the coast of Wales. The Life of St. Patrick, who lived about the middle of the fourth century, describes his capture, his life in Ireland and his ultimate escape. A steady stream of Britons emigrated to Brittany and there are many references to the depopulation of Welsh coastal villages.

It is probable that many of what are considered to be English characteristics were already fixed in the people. If so, although there would have been suppleness and a tendency to conform to the local King's commands, traditions themselves would have been slow to change and would have coexisted with the new ideas in one form or another. Rome would have become a legend, to be spoken of much as we speak of the Elizabethan age today, but family names (Arthur is probably the Latin Artorius) and certain practices must have survived. Christianity began to spread in Britain from the third century onwards but the older cults continued there for another couple of centuries.

We know something of Celtic doctrine from early Welsh poetry and Breton folklore. It seems to have had much in common with some forms of Eastern thought. Life was considered as a time of trial: if its initiation was successfully passed, the spirit rested after death until the moment came for another return to earth. This continued until, after many lives, some attained the state of spiritual perfection that admitted them to Gwenved, the "white" heaven where they became fully conscious of God. They chose, however, to return as teachers to mankind from time to time until that ultimate and future moment should come when all humanity would attain their state.

It need not surprise us to find these similarities with some forms of Buddhism. England seems to have been in contact with the East from very early times. Egyptian faïence beads have been found in Wessex graves and a probably Mycenaean dagger was discovered at Stonehenge. Irish Christianity was influenced by the austere practices of the hermits in the Egyptian deserts and rebirth itself seems to have been accepted for a time by some of the early Christian Fathers.

Wars foster change, and by the sixth century it is probable that Celtic doctrines had often become the repetition of formulas in an archaic tongue that was not easily understood. The people had to follow the religion of their King and although a change of faith probably meant little to the majority it must have been hard for the Celtic priests and for those who believed in the religion in which they had been brought up. It was truly a time of confusion because a little later they were also in conflict with the pagan North.

The story of Scilly being the islands of the dead is reported by Procopius. He was recording a legend, yet it is interesting to note that more barrows are said to have been discovered on Scilly than in the whole of

9

Cornwall and it may well have been used as a burial place for the ancient kings.

Sea travel in those days was more extensive than we used to suppose. Irish monks reached Iceland before the Vikings. They may have got as far as Greenland. The actual Norse invasions did not begin until two centuries later but men from Scotland and possibly Frisia were doubtless visiting the West as sailors and traders.

The world of research opened to me when I discovered *The Legend of Sir Gawain* by Jessie L. Weston at the age of sixteen. I had already been studying the Norman Conquest for a couple of years. It is probable that Sir Gawain was one of the original British heroes, a leech and warrior, famous for his courtesy and courage. In *Diu Krone* he was successful in the quest for the Grail and in other stories he was partially successful; he asked one question but failed to ask the second that would have restored fertility to the surrounding land. In later tales he was displaced by other figures. I was interested as a matter of history. Gawain may have been associated with what we should now call a "resistance" movement of the English under Norman rule and the Church may have disliked him because he seems to have taken over certain magical attributes from the early British gods. His real story belongs to a very early century and only traces of it remain, yet the tradition must have been a strong one because it flowered a last time in *Sir Gawain and the Green Knight,* written about the end of the fourteenth century. I have consulted, of course, many other authorities on the subject.

Those who wish to read more about those early days will find the following books, among the many that I have consulted, of great general interest.

R. J. C. Atkinson, *Stonehenge* (London, Hamish Hamilton, 1956).

Geoffrey Ashe, *From Caesar to Arthur* (London, Collins, 1960).

H. M. Chadwick, Nora K. Chadwick, and others, *Studies in Early British History* (Cambridge, The University Press, 1954).

Nora K. Chadwick, *Poetry and Letters in Early Christian Gaul* (London, Bowes & Bowes, 1955).

R. G. Collingwood and J. N. L. Myres, *Roman Britain and the English Settlements* (Oxford, Clarendon Press, 1956), 2nd ed.

T. C. Lethbridge, *Herdsmen and Hermits; Celtic Seafarers in the Northern Seas* (London, Bowes & Bowes, 1950). Essential for the voyages.

R. A. S. Macalister, *The Secret Languages of Ireland* (Cambridge, The University Press, 1937). Essential for all cloak and dagger addicts.

Eugene O'Curry, *On the Manners and Customs of the Ancient Irish* (London and New York, 1873), 3 vols. I discovered this book through a reference in the *New York Times Book Review*. It leaves one wondering if the Irish were like Homeric heroes, Red Indians or modern African tribes.

Cecile O'Rahilly, *Ireland and Wales* (London and New York, Longmans Green, 1924).

W. Y. Evans Wentz, *The Fairy-Faith in Celtic Countries* (London, Frowde, 1911).

Jessie L. Weston, *The Legend of Sir Gawain* (London, David Nutt, 1897).

—, *From Ritual to Romance* (Cambridge, The University Press, 1920). This is now fortunately available in the Doubleday Anchor paperback series, after having long been unobtainable.

Gwynn Williams, *An Introduction to Welsh Poetry* Philadelphia, Dufour, 1952).

—, *The Burning Tree* (London, Faber & Faber, 1956).

There is a vast literature on the subject but usually the other books and articles that I have read have been intended for specialists. The books listed above will be enjoyed by any who care for poetry or early history.

Finally, in order to feel the atmosphere of the time, I made a voyage from Cornwall via Wales to southern Ireland and back in a twenty-ton boat with a Diesel engine and sails. I do not pretend that this was approximate to the sailing conditions of sixth-century ships but it was very different from travel even in a small steamer and I learned a good deal more than I had expected about the roughness and the dangers of the sea.

# I

NOT a leaf stirred in the July heat. There was no sound, neither the thump of a staff nor the tapping of a messenger's sandals. I peeped cautiously through a hole in the center of the hedge and saw that the path was empty. I looked back, my companions were asleep in the Long Field, nobody had noticed me crawling up the bank. I glanced swiftly to right and left once more, scrambled through the bank and started to run towards Lestowder as fast as my legs would carry me. I should be beaten, of course, and worse still, get no supper unless I could filch something from a stall before they caught me, but an hour of freedom was worth a few blows or even a hungry night.

13

It was so unjust. Was it only two years since my uncle had come for me? It seemed a lifetime. "It is I who make the sacrifice, Honorius," my mother had pleaded while I had knelt in front of them both in supplication. I know that she had tried to save me. "You will never make a priest of him," she had protested, "he is too like his father." My heart had quickened when she had said the words because I wanted to resemble him. He had been killed at the beginning of the civil war. "But, Ruan, try to understand," my uncle had answered patiently, "there is nobody else." According to our tradition, the head priest who was unmarried was always succeeded by a nephew, and my cousin, Kadwy, who had wanted to study, had caught a fever (from it, I thought) and died. My elder brother had taken over the farm and had a wife and children. "Remember," Honorius continued a trifle haughtily, "we sit next in rank to the King and guide him in council." That was little comfort to me. I had hated school from the start. You cannot take a hunting dog from the woods and expect it to bark with joy in a kennel.

Honorius said that I had been spoilt. My mother's kinsman, Dungarth, had taken me out with him in a coracle, the herdsmen had shown me how to cut reeds and whistle the lambs back into the fold. I knew every inch of Godrevy from the wide sandy bay where we swam up to the fragrant rushes that I cut in armfuls to strew over my mother's floor. It was cold and desolate at Lestowder after our warm and happy village. My uncle was famous as far away as Wales, where they

14

usually considered a teacher to be ignorant unless he had received his white robes from one of their schools, so that my fellow pupils had come to him because they wanted to be scholars. We slept on thin pallets on a hard floor, not to train us as sailors but to subdue the flesh. I pretended every evening that it was to fit myself for a place on Dungarth's ship. I did not want to weaken my emotions. I wanted to enjoy every moment of the day with all the power of my growing body and explore the world with both senses and mind. "Death will come for us soon enough," I said to my uncle. "Not to be happy is to waste life and it is this that is sinful, it is not the roaming through the woods nor eating when you say we should fast."

It disturbed me to have no weapon training; no boy can become a good swordsman alone. The wars were over, the power of the Saxons had been broken, we had the Great Peace that the kingdoms desired. Yet we lived on the coast and the seas were full of Irish raiders while we heard every summer of fresh fighting in Gaul. One day, the old men predicted, another invasion might strike us from the east. Should such a moment come what use were the genealogies (there were hundreds of them) that I had to learn by heart? Our training took years because it was supposed to bring bad fortune to the land if our tongues stumbled over a word. What did I care if King Eudav's father were Caradoc or Bran? It was not an old man with a tottering crown who mattered to me but a girl walking up from the mill with a basket on her head or a falcon swooping downwards as fast as any wave upon the wild dove. I liked the doves as well but there were too many of them and they were good in a pie on a cold November night when we listened to real stories round a smoky log fire instead of the formal staves that we chanted at school about otherwise forgotten wars. We always knew what was coming next when Uncle Honorius opened his mouth; although he had a wonderful voice, it boomed like the waves against a solitary rock.

The first summer they had sent me home for the harvest. "Let me join Dungarth," I had begged because he was a priest of sorts as well as a sailor, being captain of the ship that took the annual tribute of grain and wine to the islands of the west. On that terrible day when the richest province of Dumnonia had sunk under the waves, only this outpost had survived. It had been spared, according to tradition, because it was the burial place of our ancient kings. We were never allowed to name it nor even to look in its direction, if its rocks were visible on a clear summer day. Dungarth and his crew had taken an oath never to reveal the course nor to speak of what they saw and, apart from them, no man who had tried to sail there had ever returned alive.

I will run away, I had promised myself every morning, but then my mother had looked at me sorrowfully and begged me to be patient and so I had lost my courage. "One day you will be second to the King," she had said, "but I shall never live to see it." I knew now that my uncle had only let me go to Godrevy because she was ill. She had died so suddenly that winter that she had been buried before a messenger could reach us. For a time afterwards I had tried to subdue my will, to make up for the thoughtless acts that are part of a boy's life and that seem to make mothers anxious, but the spring had come and gone, midsummer was here and with the year's growing I was restless. After all, the gods make us according to their will and would they have given me the heart of a kestrel if they meant me to live like a sparrow?

Oh, the days, how long they seemed! We repeated verses, we held mock courts where we spoke about law to each other in an archaic language everybody else had forgotten, we prayed interminably for the safety of the King and his land. The only endurable hours were the ones that my companions hated; we had to help water the cattle and till the fields on the farm where we lived. There were no girls, no hunting, and an incessant threat hung over us that if we did not watch things we risked bringing a famine on the land. It was true that my uncle said that mercy was a truer weapon than threats but this did not prevent Kynan, the priest in charge of us, from beating us whenever we made a slip in word or act.

What I enjoyed most was a fair and there was always a big one at Lestowder every summer. It had been my favorite day of the year because traders arrived with white and brown bales from all over the West. We were usually allowed to go in Kynan's charge to see any relatives who might come but during the morning Honorius had called us together in the courtyard and forbidden us to leave the farm. "The King has a fever," he had thundered, "and I will not have you wandering about a market place when you should be praying for his recovery. You are trained by his favor."

I ran until I was breathless but by that time I was within the shelter of the first huts. These were the usual wattle shelters daubed with mud but they were strongly built and some were new. Much of the country had not yet recovered from the years of devastation but this was the King's town and it had not been plundered. Hides swung across the entrances instead of doors but the place was empty except for a couple of hens and an old man asleep in the sun. Everybody who could walk was already at the booths.

It was the one day in the year when I could push my way without fear of recognition through the dense crowd moving towards the square. There were people here from every village within thirty miles, traders had ridden up on ponies from the two nearest ports and every inhabitant of the actual valley was either helping at a stall or strolling along the road. Dozens had slept in an open field on the other side of the town during the previous night. Men shouted offers, greeted friends or yelled at each other until the noise was as rough as if a swarm of bees had flown out of a tree trunk against an intruder.

A hand twitched my coat. I looked round anxiously, expecting to find Kynan's heavy fingers gripping my collar, but it was a barefooted girl, she was six maybe or seven, in a tattered dress that was already too small for her, holding out a necklet of shells. They were not even cowries; I liked these because the brown or black dots along the wrinkled, rosy backs helped me to count. This circlet was made from the painted tops and wentletraps that were common to all the beaches. She was too shy to say a word but jerked her head round from time to time to glance up the path: there was a toll at fair time on everything that was sold. I wished that I could give her something to buy a cake, she must be one of the cave dwellers' children and if so it was an act of extreme bravery to venture as far as Lestowder. They were wild folk, smaller and darker than we were and hated by us all. My mother had known a Godrevy woman who had left her baby in a patch of grass while she was picking blackberries not ten feet away but when she had looked up after a moment the child had disappeared. If we had found the body of a traveller who had lost his way lying below a cliff we blamed the underground people, although Honorius declared it was more likely to have been an outlaw who wanted the man's weapons. I held up my hands to show that they were empty and the child, who had been smiling at me, looked as if she were about to cry. I strode away, more resentful of my fate than ever. If I had come with my own people from our village I should have had a coin or two in my bag but here I was, a royal ward, and unable even to give alms to a beggar. Besides, it made me uneasy because a blessing from the cave dwellers was said to bring good fortune for a year.

Each trade had been allotted a space to itself in the square. The craftsmen sat with their wares in front of them in a formal pattern like the staves of a genealogy. The food stalls with their tiny braziers came first. Most men would eat once the trading was finished; they were followed by the saddlers and potters, while the merchants sat on stools in the center with their goods arranged not on the ground but on boards supported by trestles.

"Five eggs!" A man took a step forward and held up a bit of rope.

"Five eggs! For that length of thread? It wouldn't hold a toy boat on a summer day," a fellow growled in reply. He had the sailor's mark on him, a lucky shell dangling from a weatherbeaten cap. "I'll give you five cowries."

"Cowries!" There was a yell of indignation, "I wouldn't give an egg for a bag of them."

"Who has ever eaten cowries?" an innocent voice inquired from the back of the crowd and we laughed. Then as the bargaining began in earnest I smelt something strong and oily and looked round. A fisherman had come up with a string of puffins dangling from a pole balanced on his shoulder. Some people considered them a delicacy but I had shared the liberty of the rocks too often with the soft, lumbering birds and their bright orange bills to want to eat them. Doves, yes, ducks, yes, but I could no more have trapped puffins than I could return willingly to the house of the King's wards.

I wandered on, happy to have people pressing against my arms again, with their shouts and songs. A man had flung a fleece over his back to keep the heavy load that he was carrying from rubbing his coat and I saw a quantity of black specks hopping from it onto a farmer's hat. We ducked when the farmer, noticing what had happened, banged the hat against a post and swore. "Try a spike of furze," a neighbor yelled, "there's nothing like furze for beating out fleas." Why could I not continue like this—we were all so happy—instead of living cut off from the center of life? I looked up at the sky that was a hot enamel blue instead of the cloudberry color that would come with late August and wondered whether the gods really preferred our senseless chanting to the happy murmur of this contented crowd?

"Look! Look!" There were exclamations of wonder from the throng in front of us as we pressed forward in a mass towards the middle of the square. I could not see over their heads so had to wait my turn to walk past the Gaulish merchant's booth where a great bowl had been set out alone on a long plank. I had often seen vessels of an identical shape decorated with stripes but a design of animals covered this jar from its sturdy base to the rim around the top. "Look, a deer," the farmer who was still carrying his hat pointed with his stubby finger, "and this side, a doe. If it were not for the clump of bushes at her tail I could swear it was Lynn Pool, on a moonlit night."

"Ah, what do you know about Lynn Pool?" The taunting came from the back of the crowd. Lynn was part of the royal domain and only the King's foresters were supposed to hunt there. The farmer started, then he shouted back angrily, "The river mouth is open to us all and I have seen plenty of deer tracks crossing the sands."

"After your dogs have driven them into the water?" The farmer tried to elbow his way backward, yelling of course, but the crowd was sober and not yet in a fighting mood. Two men tried to pacify the poacher while others dragged the tormentor away. Lynn, Lydd, I suppose that it was the similarity of the names or because whenever I was happy the thought of my future came to frighten me. But I remembered Lydd, my uncle's fosterling, whom he had wanted to train as a messenger but who had run away before I had come to the school. I had seldom seen him and some people said that he had been a poacher of more than hares.

I took my opportunity and stopped to look at the bowl. It hardly seemed possible that a man's fingers could have made it; a thin line was enough to bring the rushes in front of me that grew near my home. It was just the moment for cutting them and I thought sadly that perhaps I should never see Godrevy again. The doe, alert for danger, lifted a tiny, white-rimmed ear that was no longer than the oval of a fallen nut. There were ripples on the water and yet the farmer was right. The bushes disturbed me, they were too large, they would not grow so near such tall trees. Then I saw a line at the end, hardly a line, it might have been an accidental scratch that wound away from the wood to the left as if it led to some crossing that we were not shown. I should have liked to lean forward and touch it but a surly-looking Breton was watching me and I kept my hands by my sides. "What do you want for it?" I heard a man ask. I knew the fellow by sight. He had a farm a mile above our mill and was said to own fifty cows.

"A gold piece or an ox." It was the merchant himself who answered. He was one of the fair-haired Gauls, taller than we were and much quieter than his restless, Breton servants.

"An ox!" The farmer stepped backwards with a laugh. "It isn't worth a sheep." Yet I was wondering how so magnificent an object could be measured in the terms of our everyday struggle with sickness and the seasons?

"But such work isn't a man's task," a shepherd objected. In spite of the heat he had a heather-colored cloak rolled across one shoulder as if he feared that it might rain. "If you gave me a thing like that I should not know what to do with it. It is only fit for a palace or church."

"A month's journey from here," the Gaul answered quietly, "there is a city ten times bigger than Lestowder where they honor a man who can make such a picture more than a farmer with ten yoke of cattle."

The crowd laughed. They took it for a joke. "Give him a pig," somebody shouted and I moved a little out of line to see if the path continued on the further side. The Gaul looked at me haughtily, he knew that I had no money. "You have seen a stag before, haven't you? Move on and let the others have their chance."

I did not want the bowl myself, the shepherd was right in a way, where could we put such a vessel in our stone or wattle huts with the cows in winter at one end of them? It was because it suggested another way of life that I still stood staring at it. Perhaps this city that the Gaul had described was free from the traditions that strangled us and if I could reach it (I felt my blood tingling with a sudden exhilaration) I could forget my ancestors and become somebody new.

The throng behind pressed me forward with them towards the next booth where a smith was holding up a sword; it was a well-balanced weapon with a long, smooth hilt. "No, I would rather have an ax," I heard the man saying next to me, "axes are better for cutting down trees."

"Who wants a sword now except the King's body-guard?"

"The Great Peace will not last forever."

"It will last my time. We taught the Saxons a lesson."

"It's the moors that protect you," another Gaul said. I recognized him as a trader who had come regularly to the fair for as long as I could remember. "And your winds. It took us three weeks this time to make harbor and we thought one day our ship was going to turn up-side down."

"Moors or winds," the first speaker shrugged his shoulders, "who cares as long as we can keep on with the plowing? It is hard enough to fill the barn without having to fight barbarians as well though they only follow their chiefs. A Saxon doesn't want to leave his farm any more than I do."

"In this world, it's the rulers who matter."

"But after the troubles at the beginning of his reign,"

the shepherd said in a loud but puzzled voice, "the King has given us peace and safe roads."

"It is not the Saxons nor even the Irish pirates," the smith answered bitterly, "sometimes it is village against village." There was an uneasy silence because every person in the square bore some scar from the civil war. My own father had been killed in a stupid ambush miles northeast of Godrevy while riding to the muster. One of his men had found his sword sticking in a clump of reeds and had brought it back to us. The fellow owed his life to his horse having gone lame so that he had lagged behind the rest. I had often looked at the sword hanging on the wall and my brother had promised to give it to me because like the man in the crowd he found an ax more useful on a farm. If I had to stay with Honorius I should lose this as well because we were not allowed to possess or handle weapons.

It was the moment when I should have been driving our cattle up from the stream and, thinking of home and of all that had been taken from me, I remembered the wretched child with her shells. Suddenly I was frightened of the future and I turned abruptly towards the potters; they were sitting on the opposite side of the market place with their everyday, familiar wares. It was rash, I knew, but if Siric was there he would give me news of my brother.

I could not find him at first, the row was full of strong, red Dumnonian jars, but I picked my way along it carefully, looking for the ocher clay that the Trebarveth men used. I stopped beside a bowl that had the familiar thong pattern underneath its handle until Siric noticed me. "Master Ruan, master Ruan," he called, "welcome, I am glad to see you." He smiled until his weatherbeaten face was as broad as his own lamps.

"Is my brother here, Siric?" I asked after I had greeted him. My fears vanished in the happiness of talking again to a man from my own village. "No," he shook his head, "he sent two men with some calves and sheep he wants to sell but you know what he is like, he would rather sit on his own bench and count his flocks than walk twenty miles to a market." I nodded agreement; my brother was a dull, plodding fellow, far more suited to be my uncle's heir than I was, but perhaps I looked too relieved because Siric added, "I did not know that you were allowed to come to the fair."

"We are not but my uncle gave me permission to come for an hour because he thought that my brother would be here." It was a lie but if Honorius would not understand how homesick I was, what else could I do?

"Can I take him a message?" Siric asked. Then, just as I was wondering what to say a farmer came up, with some fowls in a basket, and Siric turned to chant in a seller's singsong voice, "Bowls and lamps, a whole set of bowls for a single hen, jars for this season's honey, four eggs each."

"I have plenty of bowls but I will give you a bag of herbs for this lamp."

"A lamp! That size! It's worth a couple of fowls."

The man laughed and I left them to their bargaining while I slipped to the back of the pots to sit with Siric's son and listen to what Godrevy gossip he could tell me. Every word about the fishing and this friend or that was as precious to me as a crumb of cake. Eventually Siric packed one of his bigger lamps into a rough basket full of grass, and an indignant fowl was pushed into an already overcrowded coop at the potter's side. "Taking up farming?" I teased, as the buyer walked away.

"No, I shall exchange them later for some bags of meal. But your brother, what am I to say to him?"

"Tell him that I am well and that my uncle adds his greeting to mine." Siric nodded, then he said, looking at my face, "All the same, master Ruan, you are paler than you were last summer. This learning they cram into you must be hard on the head."

"Very hard," I agreed.

"If your uncle would not object, might I offer you this for water when your throat is dry after much recitation?" He held out one of his best polished bowls as humbly as if I were not a boy but an official. We were forbidden to accept gifts while we were pupils, but after all what Siric wanted was to give me pleasure, I was hungry and it would buy me a supper. "May the gods bless you," I said in the gravest imitation of my uncle, "an offering freely made brings happiness to the giver." I took the gift, bowed solemnly again and bade him farewell. "Be sure to greet my brother," I called back as I walked with slow, ceremonious steps towards a road that would have taken me back to school.

They were clearing a space for dancing opposite the tables where they were serving food and wine. As soon

27

as I was sure that Siric could not see me, I plunged into the throng again, turned and walked along the stalls until I came to a girl ladling honey sauce the color of her skin onto the hot, crescent-shaped cakes that were made only on the day of the fair. "Hungry?" She smiled at me while her father handed two pies to a farmer and his wife.

"Yes, but I have to sell my bowl before I have any pence."

"I'll give you a cake for it," she teased, keeping an eye on her father, who had his back to us.

"A cake! The bowl is worth three dinners but I'll give you a kiss for one," I joked. She was just like the dairy girls whom I had chased around the barn my last happy summer.

"You impudent child!" She pretended to hit me with her ladle.

"Two more pies." Her father was too busy serving to turn round. She reached up to take them from a basket swinging from a pole and at that unguarded moment I leaned over, kissed her, snatched a cake from the dish and ran off into the middle of the crowd again, licking the honey from my almost scalded fingers.

It was still early and it took me some time to sell Siric's gift to an old woman for a dozen fresh eggs in a rush basket. I had not expected to get more than six but I told her a sad story about losing my fair penny on the moors while I was helping to get a man's pony out of a ditch. It was wrong of course but I was going to be beaten anyhow so what did a lie or more matter? I was now at the edge of the market again and I had to walk carefully lest my elbow were jolted and I upset my precious burden. I was looking round for the nearest cook stall when I remembered the child and her necklet. It was sheer superstition but in spite of myself, or perhaps because I was at the end of the road where I had passed her, I started to look for her. One, two, three, four, I began to count my steps and fight a battle over each as to whether to continue or turn back? It was quite a distance away, of course she had already run home, I could hear the drums beating and calling me to the square but then I saw her, standing where I had left her two hours before, still holding her miserable shells. I offered her an egg, expecting to see her face light up with gratitude. She stared at me instead and shook her head. "But I won't give you a straw more than two," I said gruffly and made as if I would walk away. She snatched off the filthy rag that was round her hair and held it out, muttering something that I did not understand. I put the two eggs down, she offered me the shells, I pushed them aside but she forced them into my fingers and uttered in a hoarse, shrill whisper but in my own language, "Blessings on your voyage, sailor." Then she clutched the cloth to her chest and raced towards the moors, as fast as her legs would carry her.

I was glad now that I had returned, she had called me "sailor." It meant nothing, of course, any fisher boy was that to the cave people but it had made me feel a part of the world again instead of being my uncle's pupil. "A lamb, a sack of meal." Some plowman with enormous arms thrust a handful of grain under my nose. I ducked under a net hanging from a pole, bartered the rest of my eggs for a meat supper and half a loaf of bread and then, if I had had any sense, I should have slipped homewards before Kaden had discovered my absence. The sun was a ball of flame in an emerald sky, the pipers started, girls formed into a circle, clapping their hands, and as I thought of our room with barely a handful of rushes between my shoulders and the hard floor, a harper began softly, almost as if he were speaking to me alone, *"The West was in Gawain's blood, his cradle was our moors, other singers may tell you a different story but I know why he rode to Belerion on his last adventure to find a ship."*

The man was sitting on a rush stool, looking above our heads towards the hills, with his boy sitting cross-legged on the ground beside him. *"We Cornish are brave,"* he began, *"yet I have known a fellow afraid to cross the cliffs at night who had fought an Irish raider with a simple staff. He was wise. The darkness belongs to the earth and not to man. Now, as I was saying, Gawain knew the countryside round here as well as he knew the scratches on the blade of his sword but one night he dreamed that he was lying half in and half out of a ford, with the King's banner, ripped in two, floating in the water beside him."*

"Oh, the sad omen," the crowd muttered dutifully.

*"The following day Gawain refused to hunt. He sat down in the King's hall, pretending that an old wound troubled him, turning the dream this way and that way*

30

*in his mind, unable to decide whether it were some evil
illusion or a prophecy. Twice he opened his mouth to
speak and twice he shut it again; it is a cruel thing to
foretell a man's doom because . . ."*

"You have eaten too much cheese for supper," my
neighbor yelled; he was a red-cheeked, heavily built
farmer with a jug of beer in his hand.

We laughed. The harper frowned and shouted at us,
"Did you never hear the saying, silence is safer than
speech?" He looked proudly across our heads towards
the center of the fair ground and I wondered if he were
also thinking of the Gaulish bowl? He muttered something to his boy, waited till the noises round him had
subsided and then went on, *"Gawain could not join in
the feasting that night but went to his chamber early,
hoping that a night's sleep would drive away his fears.
Yet he dreamed again, a second time, that river water
was lapping round his neck and that a torn fringe from
the banner had fallen across his face to suffocate him."*

"He was chewing his coverlet," the farmer shouted,
"I've done the same myself after a jug of new mead."

*"The King gave a banquet the next evening,"* the
harper continued, ignoring the interruption, *"but Gawain
sat sorrowfully in his place, hardly replying to the jests
and toasts. His companions left him alone, supposing
that he had a fever or that his shield arm troubled him in
a place where there were more scars than skin over the
bone. The firelight danced on the bare wall and his life
unrolled itself in front of him like some great tapestry.
'Yes,' he murmured but so softly that the rest of the*

31

*company did not hear him, 'there is the oak where I hid when I rode to join the army thirty years ago. The woods were full of raiders then and now an unarmed farmer's boy can drive his sheep safely to any market.' The logs burnt down, the shadows danced in front of him, he drank a little of his wine and reflected that safe roads were the beginning of an empire. His companions had been more to him than brothers, yet he remembered his dream again and knew . . ."*

"He would sell a horse for too little in the morning," the farmer hiccupped, but the crowd by this time had been drawn into the mood of the story and told him in angry whispers to be quiet.

*"Now Gawain prized mercy above all virtues and as a servant piled more logs on the fire and the sparks flew upward again he saw that friend would take sword against friend in the war to be and sons would betray their parents. He did not want to sadden the company sitting round him so he excused himself, saying that he had an ague and went to lie on his pallet, in a cold room, far from the feasting and . . ."*

"Dreamed the same dream," the farmer yelled lustily, waving his now empty jug. A couple of his neighbors seized him roughly by the shoulders and hustled him out of the circle.

*"Gawain slept the night through like a child and on the following evening he decided to ask the elders to interpret what he now thought must have been a nightmare. He began to shiver as he sat down, whether with fear or a real ague I leave you to decide"*—the harper seemed

to look solemnly at each of our faces in turn—"*and he got up to warm his hands at the fire. It was the last night of the feast and nobody has seen so proud a sight since that night. He thought as he looked at the silk coats of the men and the long robes of the women that it was like a triumphant banner, blue, white and scarlet, with tassels of gold. He stooped in front of the blaze and noticed a lady sitting near him on a stool. Her green, rush-colored dress reminded him of a day when he was among the youngest of the King's warriors and had surprised a girl swimming alone in a pool. It was not a lake but the same reed-grown place that you shepherd boys go to at Manaccan. . . .*" He paused and the young men laughed.

"*Now the lady was bending over something on her lap, it was a round mirror set in a pattern of silver that had been common in his grandmother's day, but instead of a young face with an oak leaf behind the ear, an old gray-haired man looked up at him with desperate eyes. He walked back heavily to his own seat, muttering in bewilderment, 'My mother told me that I should never grow old.' He had always supposed her to mean that he would be killed in some battle while he still had his full strength. His sword arm felt heavy and instead of telling the councilors about his dream he described it to his neighbor in a quiet, almost hesitating way. This comrade was captain of a company of the King's guard and Gawain noticed that the man smiled at him a little, thinking that the mead had gone to his head. In fact, the fellow hardly listened to the end of the story, just as you get restless, my friends, when the drums call you younger ones to dancing."* The harper made a gesture across our heads but people were still busy eating and the evening music had still not begun.

*"Gawain got up slowly and not a friend in that great company called to him to stay as he walked out of the hall, past the sentries, across the courtyard and towards the building where the King's guests slept. The early stars were shining in a velvet sky but before he reached the threshold the wildest, roughest urchin that ever slipped inside a palace wall flung himself at the warrior's feet. Gawain was always courteous, as I have said, he noticed that the boy was trembling and supposed that the steward must have threatened to set the dogs on him for some small fault. 'Hast lost thy way, child?' he asked in a grave, kind voice, 'or dost thou seek thy father?'*

*"The urchin pushed the hair back from his forehead and replied in a hoarse whisper, 'The ship will be at Belerion tonight.'*

*" 'The ship! What ship?' Gawain asked suspiciously but the boy pressed a small object into his hand and darted away. It was too dark to distinguish what it was inside the doorway, so he walked back to the fire that they had kindled in the yard to warm the soldiers and replenish the torches. 'But this is my mother's brooch,' he muttered in surprise as he held it up to the light; it was a star with five red stones that he had sometimes played with as a child. The words came back to his mind that she had spoken when he had ridden away to join the King, 'You will have a harder task, Gawain, than most of your fellows but when it is over you will join me*

*again.' Then she had sighed because she knew that his
thoughts were not with her but with his new sword.
She had clutched his sleeve, he remembered, and had
added desperately, 'The messenger who comes for you
will bring my token, you marked the gold in the corner
with your teeth when you were not as long as a hunts-
man's knife and lay in my lap.' He felt the cold wind
blow through the cloak that he had flung across his
shoulders as he had left the banqueting hall, and a
dozen scenes came tumbling into his head: the first kestrel that he had seen on a falconer's wrist, a dozen pig-
lets fighting over a split sack of acorns and the yellow
flowers like butterflies on the somber rue in the leech's
garden. And remember, my listeners . . ."* the harper
looked directly at us again, *"some have said that Gawain's
mother was immortal and others that she was weary of the
world and returned to the island where she was born,
far to the west, across the sea."*

There was deep silence for a moment and if they had
driven a flock of sheep behind us we should not have
noticed either the barking dogs, the thump of a tally
stick or the dust. We were inside the story, this was part
of the magic and adventure of the fair. The harper
took a draught of water from the cup that his boy handed
up to him and then he began again, slowly and quietly,
as if he, himself, were not quite sure of the words.

*"Gawain went first to his room to arm himself and to
fetch a thicker cloak; then he roused a sleepy stable
boy to help him saddle Gringalet, his horse. The beast
neighed as they rode slowly towards the entrance and*

35

*he thought that the animal seemed to have grown younger; it had lost some fat. He stopped at the gate because he heard his comrades laughing and singing and he longed to greet them once more before the journey. Gawain sat there motionless for a couple of minutes because he knew that once he reached Belerion he would never see them again in this life. He was tempted to turn back but the brooch seemed to scorch his hand and he felt a child's fear of being disobedient and late. 'Once I won, once I lost,' he muttered and Gringalet trotted forward as if it knew the destination better than its master.*

*"It was more than three hours' ride but the wind dropped, it began to rain and they brushed against all manner of twigs and bushes in the darkness. The ground was full of holes and loose stones so that it was a marvel that they did not fall but Gawain noticed neither the jolts nor the raindrops streaming down his collar because in spite of the King's praise he was grieved at having failed the second half of his test, but of that, as you know,"* the harper paused gravely, *"I have no right to speak."*

And why not, I wanted to yell back at him but he would have ignored me as he had the farmer and the others would have turned me out of my place in the row. Yet if Gawain had failed to understand, was it not all the more essential to persevere in the search? Perhaps my uncle could have helped me but he hated storytellers. "They have no eloquence," he complained, "and their voices are rough from shouting against the wind.

I forbid you to listen to them." He might have been less severe. I did not like Kaden's measured chanting of the laws but I had to bear them patiently every day.

"*Now Gawain was lonely,*" the harper continued. "*'Oh, Gringalet,' he said to his horse, 'have we ridden all this way on some fool's errand? My judgment has gone. I am getting old.' His fingers were stiff as he groped for his sword hilt and the wounds ached along his arms. He pulled the reins gently, being tempted to return and face the mockery of his fellows for galloping out like an untried boy on so wild a night, when he heard a whistle and the waif stepped from behind a furze bush, almost in front of Gringalet's nose. 'I will lead you to the beach,' the urchin said and he trotted beside them until they came to firm sand and the splashing of small, familiar waves. The rain stopped as they reached the shingle, and the moon and the shore were the same crescent and the same color.*

"*Gawain took the token from his belt and as he lifted it he saw in a shadowy, terrible dream a madman striding with averted features the length of the King's hall to seize the ancient glass cup that they had borne to the King after every Saxon defeat. It was the emblem of the land but the figure grasped it and smashed it against a stone. Then the disk darkened, there were only fragments visible, thorns growing over the new roads, a girl's body drifting down a stream, some oak crashing over hastily buried treasure, and a friend, he recognized him by the devices on the shield, sprawled with an arrow through his throat across the heather. We tried to do too much,*

37

*he thought wearily and yet what purpose had existence otherwise?*

*"The boy touched his sleeve and Gawain saw that a little boat was coming towards them with a platform at one end, such as was used to ferry horses across rivers. Gringalet shook its wet mane and its master patted its flank . . ."* the harper made a movement with his hand and I think that we all saw the great, nervous charger standing with its hooves half covered in the loose sand. *" 'We are not to be separated,' Gawain muttered gladly but he dropped his cloak on the ground as a sign of departure to his former companions. He noticed, as it lay there on the stones, that it had the shrunken appearance of an old man whose armor had grown too large for him.*

*" 'Come,' the boy said imperiously, taking Gringalet's bridle. 'The ship is waiting for us.' Then Gawain knew that a gift had been granted to him in spite of his failures. He would not have to watch the end of the empire that he had served although he was now to leave on the most perilous of his journeys. The moonlight shone on the distant sails, the air was as warm suddenly as on a summer night and as he followed the pair towards the water his heart began to beat strongly again, as if the years had dissolved with the dreams and he were a young man going to meet his first love."*

The harper stopped speaking. Nobody moved. We were still under the spell of his voice. He put his instrument on the ground beside him and I caught a flash of a different blue from his coat where the under sleeve was patched. Such men had no easy life: the priests despised them for their lack of formal training and the farmers grumbled that they did no work in the fields. He waited a moment and then said in an ordinary, almost scornful tone, "We are mortal, my friends, whatever our stories may be. A penny for a jug of ale." His boy came towards us, a shallow basket in his hands, collecting an egg here, a fishhook there or occasionally a coin. "A penny, a penny," his master shouted; he could see the interior of the basket from the platform where he stood. "If my story has pleased you I will tell you how Gawain found his youth again in the islands of happiness, as soon as I have cooled my throat."

I had spent all I had on my supper and to my shame I had nothing to give. My training had already made me critical. I had noticed slurred phrases and too familiar words. Yet something of the mystery still roared in my ears like the sound of the sea in a shell. The boy came along our line, looking hungrier than we felt after one of our fasts. I searched through my wallet but all that I could find was the necklet that the waif had sold to me. I dropped the wretched offering in the basket and walked, as swiftly as possible, towards the market place.

They were beginning to clear the stalls away so as to leave a large, clear space for the dancing. A man strolled past with a sleepy child in a red coat lolling on his shoulder. People took hands and the apple-green headcloths of the girls bobbed towards us as they circled the square. A shepherd knocked a sheaf of rushes over and grinned foolishly; they rolled a drunken fisherman to safety behind a cask. The girl from whom I had stolen a cake caught a yellow shawl as it floated from a companion's head and tossed it back to her. "Join us!" The late comers, from a grandmother in a long, patched skirt to a boy who was hardly big enough to stand on his own two legs, linked themselves on to the nearest ring. The harper put his hand to his ear as I looked round, no voice could have made itself heard above the noise. The emerald had changed to gold in the evening sky; tomorrow we began our daily patterns once more but tonight was our story, to live it as we pleased. "Join us!" A girl snatched my wrist, many were singing, an untied ribbon and a lock of black hair caught my cheek as we drew nearer to each other. I saw a Godrevy face in the distance, Siric's son grinned at me as he passed.

We heard a command. The drums stopped, the couples in front took a step forward and halted. "What is it?" somebody whispered but nobody answered him. All that I could see between my companions' heads was a wisp of dust. Somehow the crowd opened and the bodyguard came marching through the center of the square with their spear points held towards the ground. Even then I did not realize what had happened. They were almost abreast of us before a woman screamed, "The King is dead!" and began to sob. "But he only had a slight fever," the man said next to me in an uncomprehending voice. "Our harvest will fail," one after the other the women dropped to their knees, "Save us from famine! Save us from hunger!" The foreign traders bundled their goods together and began to disperse lest they were accused of bringing bad luck to the town.

"Couldn't they have let us have our feast and told us tomorrow?" a piper muttered. "I am alive and I have to eat." At that moment a harsh, familiar hand gripped my collar. "So you are here!" Kaden growled, shaking me as he pulled me after him up the road, "dancing with the girls while your master was lying dead in the palace! Wait till your uncle knows."

"You have disgraced our family, Ruan," my uncle said gravely. "I knew that you were willful but I did not expect such disobedience while the King was dying. Had you forgotten that you were his ward?"

"You will never make a priest of me." The words burst desperately from my lips before I could stop them.

"You may never have the chance to be one." I could not help being awed by my uncle's face: he had been awake all night saying the ceremonial prayers but in his full, white robes he looked more of a ruler than his master. "The Christians have the ear of the young King."

"Not those Irish monks?" They were a mysterious group who said that they had been shipwrecked during a voyage to Brittany although the country folk pretended that they had drifted ashore on a clover-leaf-shaped raft. Out of pure kindness the old King had given them a piece of waste ground. They had built a couple of huts and tilled the fields for a year or two until a night when the prince had lost his way in the fog and they had found and sheltered him. Nobody knew what they had said to him but he had given them leave afterwards to wander up and down the land, preaching their doctrines. Yet if they had so much influence and this was the first time that my uncle had admitted being actually afraid of them, was it not an additional reason for letting me abandon a training that I hated? I wriggled my shoulders hopefully as if by the sheer movement I could escape into the sunshine.

"They came as beggars and now they are as powerful as we are," Honorius continued gloomily, "though not even the seers know how long we have served the rulers of this land."

"Perhaps now that the prince is King he will send them away?" Yet as I spoke I wondered how the wild youth that I had often seen galloping across the meadows on a black horse could be our ruler? His attendants feared his moods. Sometimes he would pray for nights on end and then, just as suddenly, he would ride away to hunt and feast until his followers brought him back, days later, with torn clothes and drunken, staring eyes. It was the same with his friends. He would pick out a man for no apparent reason and treat him as a brother and after a few months, just as unpredictably, send him away. "The boy is young," people had said but as he grew older their tolerance had changed to mutterings of dislike and the councillors complained that he could not be trusted.

"They have bound him with the spell of their words," Honorius said sadly, "so it is all the more important, Ruan, that you should watch every act. The Christians reproach us for being wealthy and powerful and they have won many of the ignorant through such arguments."

42

I glanced round the room. No cell could have been more austere. Honorius held the second rank in the kingdom after its ruler but a servant could have complained that the pallet was too thin and the coverlet too patched. There was not even a curtain to keep the draft from the door and the place was bare, apart from a table and a stool. "I would do anything to serve you," I pleaded, "but I cannot give you my life."

"You are no longer a child, Ruan. What evil recklessness drove you yesterday, of all days, to that fair?"

I stood there sulkily, shuffling my feet. Honorius was old, he had forgotten what the warm, gay booths were like where every man joked with his neighbor and he had fasted so often that a slice of hot meat pie (oh, I wanted one so much that I could have cried with hunger for it) was now too rich for him. "Let me go home," I begged, kneeling and touching the hem of his robe in supplication, "let me go home."

"I have not been lucky in my wards," Honorius said bitterly, "Lydd also ran away."

It was the first time since I had come to Lestowder that my uncle had uttered the name. It was some years since he had disappeared but my uncle had once brought him to Godrevy while I was still a child and I was unlikely to forget him because he had snatched up my toy boat for no apparent reason and flung it into the sea.

"Did you actually find him in a wood?" I asked. We were forbidden to mention Lydd but I was in such disgrace that now it did not seem to matter.

"Yes, I was riding back after blessing a new farm

43

when my pony shied at a dark object lying on the path. I dismounted and found a baby, not more than a week old, lying under an oak. Nobody else would have passed that way, it was growing dusk and in another hour the wildcats would have come out. I should not have left him in any case but as he was inside the shadow of the sacred tree I supposed that it was a sign he was to grow up a priest. I took him to a forester's wife and gave her a piece of silver to nurse the baby. When he was old enough to study I brought him here."

"Did you ever discover who his parents were?"

"I think I know but I have no proof. Do you remember Lydd's hair? I believe you saw him once. It was so thick that he could never keep a cap on his head. A man had been killed in a quarrel with his neighbors a little earlier near the spot where I found the child. The man's nickname had been 'Bare Ears' because he had never worn a hood, even in winter. The mother must have been a farmer's daughter. He may have surprised her in a field or she may have gone to him willingly. Yet the boy was clever, for all his faults."

I stared at the ground. I was punished for a short truancy in the middle of a crowded fair. My uncle had been far more foolish. People had smiled at Godrevy whenever the boy was mentioned and my mother had had to slap a maid's ears for whispering in the dairy that my uncle was Lydd's father.

"You can put your mind at rest, Ruan," Honorius continued sharply, as if he were reading my thoughts, "it was a pure act of mercy. Lydd was no kin of mine."

"Yet you blame me for going off for one short hour to see my brother!"

"It was more than three hours and you were listening to a storyteller. If many people noticed you, they can say that such conduct while the King was dying was an evil omen for the land."

There were heavy footsteps outside and Kaden came in with a jug of fresh water. "You must rest," he said firmly to my uncle. "Shall I take the boy away?"

My uncle shook his head, "No, I have not finished speaking to him." I could see my companions unrolling on the grass the black clothes that would be needed for the burial. The minutes were slipping away and this might be the last chance I should ever have to persuade my uncle to set me free. I could follow Lydd's example, I knew, and run away but then I should lose Godrevy and my home.

"The people loved the old King and the prince is cunning enough to realize that they might refuse to recognize him unless he pays the proper honors to the body. He has commanded that his father is to be buried with all the traditional rites. He will wait until he is crowned before he gives his favors to our enemies but remember, Ruan, an island burial will take me from the Court and from his ear for at least six weeks."

I nodded sullenly. Why should these ceremonies matter to me? I was wondering at the moment what had happened to Lydd.

"I cannot send you home, Ruan. There is no one else in our family to succeed me in my office and if we have to face persecution and danger I shall expect you to meet it as bravely as if you stood in the shield wall. I do not want to leave you here, however, to remind the villagers that you were strolling round the market place at the time of their King's death. Dungarth's brother is sailing tomorrow to warn the islanders to prepare for the burial and he will take you with him. When did you last eat?"

"Yesterday evening," I said hopefully because I was very, very hungry.

"Good. The oath never to reveal the way has to be taken fasting. I do not wish you to return to your companions so you may remain here and think over what I have told you until sunset. You can run the wildness out of your legs as long as we are in the Scillys, for that is their hidden name," my uncle continued, smiling at me, "but when the time comes to return, your boy's dreams must be buried in their sands. And now," he pointed to the bench outside the door, "you can sit outside and wait until Kaden is ready. He will take you to the altar as soon as it grows dark."

The islands sparkled in the morning sun. Ennis Mor, the main island, Agnas, where the burials took place, Innishaw and half a dozen others floated on the sea like a buckler's rim with the silver hand grip of the Sound holding them together. We drew near to a quay of rough stones at the side of a sheltered bay. It was packed with islanders standing as closely together as mackerel in a shoal but they had left a place clear for the elders in the middle. It was not mere strangeness nor the sense

46

of adventure that I had felt, riding across the moors and through unfamiliar villages on our way to the port. This was another and an ancient land. It was the harper's landscape, whatever Honorius might say, and the boys leaping and running across the dry heather in front of us towards the bright, green ocean came straight out of the story that I had listened to at the fair. "Oh," I said as our stone anchor fell with a plop towards the sand, "look at the men! They are wearing skirts."

"They have not changed the fashion of their clothes since my grandfather's time," the captain said at my elbow. "He believed that those long coats went back to the time of the Roman garrison. They tuck them through their belts when they walk and of course the young men out in the boats wear the same jackets that we do. You will find that a lot of their customs are different from our own." He shaded his eyes from the sun and pointed towards the shore. "Can you see the man with the white hair? He is the seer from Peninnis and holds the same position here that your uncle has on the mainland. They know the news, I think, they are in their black robes."

Lines of women and children had formed a semicircle on the beach. The arrival of a ship meant not only news to them but food. I should have expected to hear some murmur of voices from the crowds but though they moved there was no sound. I wondered, almost in panic, if they could be living folk like ourselves?

"You may come with me," the captain said as two of the sailors lowered the coracle that we carried into the water, "but remember you must not land until I have

47

gone ashore alone and delivered my message. The elders will then announce the news to the people; and be careful afterwards, there will be an immediate rush for the boat. They will want to know how much timber we can give them for a pig and whether we have brought the tribute of wheat. I am sorry for them, it is cold during the winter gales and they have only driftwood for their fires or a stone lamp full of fish oil; it gives out quite a lot of heat, to warm their huts."

I shall never forget the terrifying silence as we rowed ashore. How could people and particularly children keep so still? There were rough steps in front of us; a ribbon of green weed and limpets the shape of the boss in my father's old shield were clinging to the wall. A boy a little younger than myself was waiting to grasp our scow as we drew alongside. He smiled but he did not speak. Our captain sprang out warily onto the slippery stones and scrambled up the side of the quay. I had an uneasy feeling that the tale might end when the harper called for ale and that I should wake up and find myself back at Lestowder or that at the sound of a word they would turn and throw us back into the sea. At Godrevy, if a vessel had missed its way in the fog and come into the cove, we had rushed down the beach, shouting and laughing, and calling out to the sailors as we splashed towards it through shallow water. I could not see our leader but I could hear the rumbles of words above my head. There was a pause. A voice proclaimed the death of the King, it must be the seer because the voice was trained and clear like that of my uncle although it had a different intonation, a wail passed through the crowd, there was a shout and then it was just as if a bout had ended at the wrestling grounds and the favorite had won, the multitude came to life and began to shout and talk at once.

"Welcome," the boy held out his hand to help me from the coracle. "My name is Erbin and our headman is my father. How was the wind?" He grinned because I was still looking seasick. "Have you had a good voyage?"

We were sailing over a sea so smooth that it was hard to remember that the autumn gales could bring shipwreck inside even the anchorage. The netted ripples where the light struck the surface of the water made a winding path between the scattered rocks. I had discovered no traces of the harper's island but I had found a friend. Erbin and I had been inseparable from the moment of landing. I had gone fishing with him and he had taken me in his coracle to Innishaw with a message from his father to the headman and it was he who had suggested sailing out this morning to the eastern end of the Sound to watch Dungarth arrive. It was so clear that we could just see a spiral of smoke on the mainland; it was the signal that the vessel had left.

"The ship ought to round the Point at any moment," Erbin said, loosening the rope that held our sail. "I expect you will be glad to see your uncle," he added politely.

I shook my head. It was a little more than a week since

49

I had left Lestowder but the thought of it was like a childhood fever, forgotten until a taste of sickness reminded me that it could return. "He wants to make a priest of me," I wailed.

"You a priest!" Erbin burst out laughing. "It would be the spoiling of a natural sailor. Considering that you have only been out with the fishermen in, where was it, Godrevy Bay, you haven't made many mistakes. You could sail this boat alone once you have learned our landmarks; here," with great generosity he handed me the rope to hold, "you will know as much about her as I do by the end of the summer."

"Impossible," I said firmly, only a boy whose cradle had been a coracle could understand so much about the sea. He turned into a seal whenever he dived or came up in some unexpected spot with only his head above the water. "But if my uncle talks to you," I pleaded, "beg him to let me stay. I cannot endure Lestowder again."

"Whatever made him think that you could be a priest? Was it your mother's wish?"

"No, nephew has succeeded uncle for generations in our family and the stupid boy who was to have followed him got a fever and died. I think the genealogies affected his head." I spat the words out and shuddered. "We have to learn fifty of them by heart."

"Fifty!" Erbin whistled. "Can you?" he asked.

"I know seven," I said with some pride in spite of my hatred of them; "next year we have to learn another fifteen and if we mispronounce a word it's unlucky, so Kaden thrashes us. And what use are they to anybody?

You can't make bait from them, they won't catch fish."

"It's a high position," Erbin answered, looking at me with some awe. "If you are the only one left in your family you will have to learn them all the same, we have to keep the laws."

"The yoke has been light on your shoulders," I said angrily and scooping up some water in my hands I threw it in his face just as a gust of wind caught our sail.

"Give me that rope," Erbin spluttered as he snatched it out of my hand. "You will capsize the boat if you are not more careful and if you wet my new jacket I shall tell your uncle he is right, you are only fit to be a priest. Besides, the genealogies are necessary in spite of what you say. How would it be possible to seat a stranger at our table unless we knew his rank?"

"Is it true that you heard about the King's death before we landed?" I asked quickly because though Erbin was not as angry as he pretended it was wiser to change the subject.

"Of course. The seer at Peninnis saw a black sail in a dream. He is good, he warns us sometimes about gales."

"It is strange how few even among priests have this gift. To me, as to most of us, the future is a blank wall."

"We each have our own tasks," Erbin answered indifferently, steering the boat a little nearer to the shore. "It is just as easy for our seer to have visions as for me to bait a hook."

"But do you never wonder why this sense is given to some and not to others?"

"No, there are men who say that they wish he would

tell them where the mackerel are but then we should lose the excitement of looking for them and our skill with the winds."

I nodded in agreement and yet how wonderful it would be if I knew at this moment that I should never have to sit in front of Kaden's harsh face again. Three puffins waddled down a strip of sand in front of us no wider than a sword, their orange beaks posed gravely on their thick, white breasts. I dabbled my fingers in a banded cockleshell of water that was emerald or purple, as we drifted above sand or weed. We could smell the bracken on the nearest islet and even a patch of camomile but I could not enjoy these glories because of my fears. "Let me have the rope again," I pleaded restlessly, "I will be very careful."

"Not until we have rounded that rock."

A cormorant rose into the sky, a ribbon of sea grass floated past the side, July was short, oh, why must men spoil such a summer with their narrowness? The gulls sought other feeding places, following the shoals, and change was life. What were the amulets of our great grandfathers but fetters to our younger selves?

"Look!" Erbin leaned forward eagerly. "Here she comes."

I thought at first that it was a bird. The black, old-fashioned sail obliterated all but the bow and the vessel seemed to float through the silver water as if impelled by some mysterious force towards its anchorage. We were still too far away to distinguish one figure from the other but the sunlight caught the purple cloth draped over the bier as the ship shifted a point to catch the wind. Was it true that the King was the embodiment of his race? I had seen him walk across the courtyard at Lestowder in an old frieze coat that might have belonged to one of his shepherds. What did he know now of the pomp surrounding his burial? It took a thousand shells, found only in a single bay in Ireland, to dye one yard of that purple that he had never worn during his life. He had won no victories, nobody would evoke his name during a song, but after the civil war he had endured the famine with the rest of his people and had tried to unite the survivors from both sides into a sullen, uneasy peace.

I could recognize Honorius now—he was standing beside the body—but we could not hear the prayers. The soldiers stood with their heads bent over their shields. The ship glided past us as if in a dream, no figures moved, there were only the tiny, tattering sounds of a sail straining against its ropes. The wash set our craft tossing on the waves, without a word Erbin turned our bow towards the harbor and suddenly, magnificently, although it was full daylight, a beacon blazed at the top of every large island, as if to celebrate a victory, not a burial.

The pyre had been built on a headland that was joined to Agnas by a causeway that could only be crossed at low tide. Otherwise they formed two separate islands and it was said that the water racing across the bar had the magical transparency of the great, green stones in the seer's necklace. Women dipped their babies there because it was supposed to preserve them from drowning once they were men. The priests themselves never crossed to the far hill except for burials or to light the fires of remembrance for the dead, at the time of the autumn gales.

It was hot. I knew that Erbin wanted to swim but he kept the rites more seriously than I did and if he spoke it was only in a whisper. I ran my fingers idly over the tassels of a strange plant that was creeping over the shingle where we sat and wondered if it were also some sacred flower? It was the dark blue of a deep wave caught by sunlight. "Ocean holly," Erbin murmured, noticing my interest, "we find it here and in a couple of other places." It was not like the red berries of the bushes in Lestowder wood and although the leaves were prickly they did not sting. I wondered if they were always soft and had simply stiffened in the air after pushing up from a mess of wet grit to the surface.

"He was a great ruler," a fisherman muttered, relacing his shoes. The fellow had either forgotten or had not heard that it was said on the mainland that the King owed his crown less to his courage, though it was admitted that he was brave, than to the fact that he had been the only man of rank left alive at the end of the war.

"He seized no man's inheritance, he was like a priest."

Half of the inhabitants of Agnas were grouped round us and although the King might seem a hermit to them he resembled Honorius neither in word nor in deed. I thought of my uncle's hard blue eyes staring up at the sky as if he were in a trance while his lips ordered me to repeat fifty lines aloud because I had stumbled over a word, one little, tiny word, in my recitation. Sometimes I had wondered if there was not a streak of cruelty hidden under his gentleness?

"I wish they had chosen a spot away from that headland," Erbin said in his ordinary voice, kicking some empty limpet shells with his toe.

"The other rocks were too small, the seer himself measured them."

"It is only a saying," an old man said reprovingly, "not a tradition."

I looked at Erbin, but before he could answer, the smith, who was sitting opposite us in the leather apron of his trade, turned his head towards me and explained. "They say, and I believe it myself, that whoever is laid at the top of that hill will be the last King to be buried here."

It was like a torch in a doorway on a foggy night. I knew instantly in some inner corner of my mind that it was true and only my loyalty to Honorius stopped me from saying that Constantine intended to be baptized. Some of the men from Ennor shook their heads, however, and Erbin's cousin who had sailed us over in his fishing boat that morning grunted angrily, "Stick to your forge and what you know. The place was chosen according to the omens and your own priest was satisfied. It's only a woman's tale."

There was a roar of laughter because the Agnas wives were said to be as bold as their husbands. They had to be. The seas were such that they were often isolated and short of food for months at a time. Some of the younger men began to argue about their families and the shoemaker said slyly to end the dispute, "A radish root keeps a woman from chattering, why didn't you bring some with you? We can't grow them here."

It was a favorite proverb and a fellow was answering loudly, "The biggest radish never stopped a girl's mouth," when he was hushed. A youth on the top of the hill behind us had waved his arm twice. It was the signal that the ship was in sight. I wriggled up to a rock to get a better view and Erbin followed me. "They can say what they like," he said, looking at me anxiously (I think he hoped that I would reassure him), "we believe the prophecy at Ennor too."

I was tempted to tell him about my own fears but I had promised to be silent. I murmured instead as if I had not heard him, "I'm so hungry." We had had to fast since sunset of the previous day.

"We shall feast tonight. There will be lobsters."

"And prayers." They would recite the King's deeds in full to us for the last time. "Besides, it will be dusk before the flames die down and we can sail for Ennor."

"The wind should be right. It will only take an hour."

"Suppose they wait until the pyre burns itself out?"

"Oh, they never do that," Erbin seemed shocked by my question, "they will leave some guards to watch it but we hurry home on account of the storm."

"What storm?" The tide was going down rapidly and there was hardly a ripple along the beach.

"Do you never learn anything but lists of ancestors? There is always a gale. It is the three-day salute to the warrior while he travels to the island of the dead."

"Like Gawain."

"Who was he?" Erbin looked startled, he had obviously never heard the name before.

"A leader of ours who died just before the civil war."

"He is not buried here. I do not know your genealogies but I can tell you the names of thirty kings who are lying on the headland."

"He is not a king though he did a king's work." Did Honorius despise the tale because of his scorn of wandering storytellers or was there another reason? Had Gawain also been a rebel and was his search a whisper to bring us happiness when the yoke of priest and ruler hung heavily on our shoulders? I smiled at my discovery and closed my eyes; it was a drowsy day with bees humming in the heather at my back and the sun scorching my bare wrists.

"The ship!" Erbin's shout startled me before I had had really time to fall asleep. The soldiers were lined up in front of the bier and I could see Honorius standing in front of the other priests. The light caught the links of the golden collar that was the emblem of his office and dazzled our eyes as we watched them approach. I heard a brief order; slowly, majestically the sail slid, again as if by its own volition in a billowing darkness from the yards. The anchor splashed, the men turned to lift the body and while they rowed silently towards the shore in the small boat that had gone to meet them we formed up at the end of the causeway ready to follow them to the top of the hill.

There was nothing beyond the cliff but water. There were neither islands nor rocks but only the ocean, an immense expanse that, like the King's death, ended in mystery. Perhaps Gawain had sailed across it to his mother, perhaps its end was the dwelling place of the gods, or did it roll remorselessly on, in the way thoughts creep that frighten us, in some alternating pattern of tranquillity and storm?

The barrow was built on the topmost edge. It was far enough inland so that the spray could not hammer a loose stone out of place but it was also set exactly in the center as if it were intended to be a beacon. Once the long slab had been placed on top, it would become part of the rocky wall; the heather would grow to its verge in a year or two and only the watchman on the landward side would know that it was a tomb.

Dungarth and I followed the priests at the head of the procession because we both carried objects that would be needed during the ceremony. I could see the pyre between the heads of the men climbing in front of me and the great jar into which they would put the ashes at its side. Luckily there was no wind. Erbin had told me that the flames had once set the bushes afire and the assembly had had to scramble down the scorching hillside before the ceremony had finished. Honorius held up his arm. We stopped in front of a small altar that had been set up within the shelter of a boulder and the elders beside us formed themselves into as even a half circle as possible, on the tufts of thrift and humps of broken rock. They had drawn the hoods of their black cloaks over their heads and looked like a ring of crows.

I was supposed to keep my eyes fixed on the ground but I risked a swift glance back across the slope. The last group of people was just leaving the beach; these were the onlookers, the men and women from Agnas and the other islands, who would stand respectfully a certain distance away. Erbin and half a dozen youths, all the sons of chiefs, were at my heels, with the grave gifts in their hands. A metal stud clanked against a pebble as the eight soldiers took their places behind the piled up timber. All of them were elderly men and as the sunlight caught the rings sewn to the shoulders of their leather coats I wondered what it meant to them to come to the forbidden islands and if an oath could take away a lifetime's fears? "They know they are here by lawful order," my uncle had said when I had questioned him, "why should they be afraid?" Yet once back on the mainland it would be easy for them to forget their oaths of silence and risk the anger of the gods through some simple slip of the tongue; or would they return, gravely and stiffly, with their wooden faces to their homes and remember no more about the islands than their ruler?

The Agnas men had the right to carry the bier and they came slowly forward to set it down in front of the priests. The folds of their old-fashioned clothes were tucked into their belts and I think that we all noticed the contrast between the taut muscles of their tanned

59

legs and the burden that they carried. The scarlet folds of a warrior's cloak draped the King's body for a last time. Like its master, the garment had had its history. It had been no new mantle woven by his daughters in the palace but a cloth snatched hastily from some store-room for the King's coronation. It was at the end of the famine, there had been nothing but a few crusts to give the beggars and a meager dish of meat for the royal feast. The old women at Lestowder said that it had belonged to an earlier and greater King who had been fetched to the gods without a proper burial but Kynan swore that it was a cloth of no particular value. Certainly it had never been worn beneath the Standard. The King had done his fighting in a homespun jacket, slithering through reeds and hiding in thickets. He himself had never taken it in his hand except once a year for the Midsummer feast when it had hung wearily from his shoulders as if, as people said, he did not value it. Now it would go to the fire with him, with a stain of oil on the collar and a place rubbed thin by the scabbard of a sword. It had been sewn for a ceremony and it was fitting that it should end at one. It had never been worn to draw a girl under its folds nor to keep the night air from a hunter's back. Then suddenly, in place of the shadowy figure that I had so briefly and infrequently seen, I thought of Honorius. What a ruler he would have made! The monks and shipwrecked sailors would have been fed and sheltered but afterwards he would have sent them on their way, he would not have given them land. I could imagine him riding along the borders instead

until he had won the leaders of the neighboring terri-
tories back into the ancient kingdom and united us once
more against fresh Saxon raids.

The men stepped aside for the priests from Peninnis
to begin the prayers. They spoke of the journey of the
soul from the wrestling grounds of existence to a summer haven where it rested for a time. Yet all I could feel
as I looked at the bier was mortality. We hoped that the
King would feast and dream. We did not know.

Honorius walked over to the body in his turn.

*"Bran, son of the sailor, Llyr . . ."*

As the names of the King's ancestors rang out, almost
as if they were a challenge to the sea, I had to surrender,
in spite of myself, to the beauty of my uncle's declama-
tion. I had never heard so magnificent a voice. Oh, if
they would only keep the genealogies for such a moment,
I could love instead of resenting them. Perhaps it was
the scene, the elders with their hands folded under
their cloaks, the dark moss struggling against the stubby
lichen in the rocks, the wave rolling in a long, blue wing
between us and the opposite shore, but I felt, fanciful
though it seemed, that the King's forefathers really were
near us, waiting to escort him home. The words were a
story as magnificent as any that the harpers told. The
earliest kings had driven off the wildcats and fought
the snakes with tiny, flint-tipped darts. They still kept
such a javelin within the palace. Another had led his followers against the legions, hurling torches at the pali-
sades. Each ancestor in turn had added land and riches
to the kingdom until the Saxon invasion and the civil war

61

had emptied the treasury and ravaged the fields. The folk was tired; but once the bitterness was over and the feuds were forgotten, we should be young again and grow as in my grandfather's time.

The names ended. Erbin touched my sleeve. He dared not speak but his lips formed the word "Come" as he walked slowly forward with the ritual bowl of milk. Honorius lifted the offering and as he poured it over the altar he began the prayers for the safety of the flocks left without a herdsman until the next king was crowned. Kaden had trained us well and I dared not venture to look at my uncle's face as I handed him the jar of honey that was not only a symbol of wealth as he spilt it over the stones but also of the power of eloquence to temper judgment with mercy.

We stepped back. Erbin's companions laid the grave offerings at each corner while the soldiers set the bier in the center of the pyre. There was a patch of bare earth at our feet where the logs had scraped away the grass when they had been hauled up on the previous evening. The gulls rose and we waited in an uneasy silence while they fanned some wood behind us to light the torches.

*"May you recognize your dreams on the way to
Gwenved."*

Honorius spoke the final words and I knew, although he himself might have denied it, that he was thinking of himself as well as of his friend. The day was so clear that the elderly people who had not been able to follow us across the causeway must have heard us joining in the lament. The island priests, with flaming sticks in their hands, walked to the headland and thrust them into the timber. The fire shot into the sky, the vases toppled, wine hissed over the red-hot brushwood, the heat drove us back but we could smell cloth, leather and the bitter, unfamiliar scents of the embalming ointments. The breeze carried scraps of the mantle flaming into the air but either the sword was hidden by smoke or it had sunk into the embers. It was so terrible a sight that its magnificence isolated us from grief. Destiny awarded loneliness to a ruler: there was not the touch of friendly, familiar hands carrying a fisherman to his humble burial and placing a dozen worn fishhooks and his blunt and much used knife beside him on the rocks.

The sea itself seemed to stir; perhaps it was imagination but I thought that I heard the slapping of the waves rise to mingle with our cry of farewell and we shut our eyes while the priests from Peninnis pronounced the curse upon any man who willfully disturbed the tomb. We stood for a moment in silence and then as if we knew that we had no further right to remain on the island I followed Erbin hastily down the slope towards the causeway. It was already thick with islanders hurrying back to the harbor or their boats before we were cut off by the tide.


"Wake up! Ruan, wake up!" It sounded like Erbin's voice and I must be dreaming about him as I lay at the bottom of this deep, warm cave where only I knew that I was asleep. "Wake up!" It was a faintly unpleasant echo that I tried not to hear. "Wake up!" A hand pulled my old woollen cloak away from my legs and shook me violently. I rolled over, rubbed my eyes and yawned. I could just distinguish some familiar objects, a coat hanging from a nail, the water jug on the floor, but Erbin would not let me rest. "Hurry! Where are your shoes? It's a wreck."

"A wreck?" How could there be? The course was secret and nobody knew the channel. "A wreck?" I muttered again stupidly, pulling my shoes on all the same, "Where is it? And what ship?"

"She's out to westward, blown here by the gale." The wind whistled sharply through the open door and I reached instinctively for my covers again. "Tuck in that strap and come," Erbin said impatiently, "if my cousins from Longbeach get there first they will take our coracle."

I was still hardly awake as I followed him down the narrow, slippery path that was a short cut to the harbor. Two men rushed past us, carrying long sticks. They had lit the beacon on Peninnis but a little light was already creeping into the sky. Another spurt of fire rose on Innishaw and then died down, a trailing bramble cut across Erbin's leg and he yelped, a sailor raced past us shouting, "Dungarth? Where have you got to? Dungarth . . .!"

Our end of the beach was usually empty but it was crowded now with women and children. "How did they hear?" I panted, astonished that the settlement should turn out to the newest baby at such an hour. "They lit the beacon on Agnas," Erbin answered patiently as if he were humoring a fool, as indeed he was; we lit fires on the mainland if a ship went on the rocks but I was still drowsy and preoccupied with picking my way over the rough ground.

"Bring some timber back with you," a woman shouted to us, "we need it."

"They'll be lucky if they find a couple of mackerel," her neighbor growled.

"Be careful with that stick." A mother slapped a small boy who was slashing wildly at the thistles as they ran and he howled.

What a scene it was! The sand was the greenish white of a crab's belly in the not quite dawn light, a torch here and there picked out the droop of a hood or the sharp line of a nose, otherwise the crowd was a block of shadows. One woman had wound a faded yellow cloth so tightly round her head that only her eyes were visible. "It's cold." A girl stamped the ground with her bare feet, jumping up and down to keep warm. "It's a long time since we had a wreck," the fisherman at my elbow muttered joyfully as if it were an unexpected feast while a puppy, barking frantically, rushed round the ring of people, looking for its owner. A boy held his torch up so that we could find our oars. We kept them in a hut where the fishermen stored bait, old baskets and chips of wood.

"Hurry," Erbin shouted, "the Longbeach people are coming." He launched the boat and sprang lightly on board. I followed rather awkwardly, splashing him as I took my seat, and he swore. A man yelled at us to let him come as well, we pretended not to hear and rowed off towards the Sound. Wherever we looked there were points of light as people streamed towards the wharf from farms all over the island. "Don't forget the timber," the woman yelled again to no boat in particular and as we reached the end of the quay we heard the froglike plop of a stone anchor slipping back into the water. "Somebody is going to get cursed for that," Erbin said cheerfully, "but it's good for us, the small boats will get there first."

"What are the laws here?" I asked as we hoisted our sail. The storm had blown itself out but there was a heavy undertow as we reached the open water and I was glad that Erbin was steering because it was hard to keep our bow to the waves.

"If a ship goes ashore on an island it belongs to the inhabitants, but if it is out on the open rocks then all of us share. Of course," I could feel the joy in Erbin's voice though at that moment the sail hid his face, "a man has the right to take anything that floats. I've brought two hooks."

"Suppose the crew lands?"

"Survivors are rare, you've seen our rocks. All the same, we once found some fishermen who had drifted in the fog to the back of Teän. They were Cornish and as they had landed in a calm against their will we let them take the oath of secrecy at Peninnis and sent them back with Dungarth on his next voyage. If the men are strangers, we leave them to the sea that washed them here."

"It seems terrible to throw them back into the water,

just as they think they are safe." I remembered a man whom we had found on Godrevy beach with a blue face and chattering teeth. It had been three days before he had come to his wits enough to tell us his story.

"So your priest's training has marked you after all," Erbin said with scorn. "How can we let them live? Not all the Irish follow our gods and once they know the way here the Sound would be a nest of raiders and we should be drowned ourselves or slaves."

I nodded, it was a fact. A fellow pupil of mine at Lestowder had told us about seven villages known to his kinsfolk on the coast of Wales. "The raiders burnt the houses," he had told us angrily and even Kaden had not reproved him, "where they grew barley is a wilderness of bracken and the few survivors fled inland." It would be easy for one of these captains to fire Godrevy, seize and sell my friends and wait off Innishaw until it was time for another raid, yet how could I bear to watch some wretched sailor swim ashore only to be flung back into the ocean through the justified fears of his fellow men?

We could not hoist our sail until we were well outside the harbor but the long row warmed us and I reflected dismally that we had forgotten to bring a bag of food. Everything had been washed clean by the storm and the sun rose on a world of silver islands and green glittering seas. The surface seemed smooth enough to the eye but the gale had left an undertow behind that rocked our boat and drove occasional spurts of spray across the bow. Once a butterfly blew past us towards the shore; its wings were a frailer, more transparent white than the crests below it and I wondered if it would survive to land again on some familiar plant? Erbin heard a thump and picked up an oar. A seal was watching us with the placid gaze of a sleepy dog but so heavy a beast could upset our light scow and he yelled and splashed until, its curiosity satisfied, it rolled over and dived away.

We left Agnas on our left and sailed forward to the mackerel shoals, a remote, desolate place where we bobbed on the water like a bit of driftwood. It was cold to the touch when I trailed my hand overside and must be deep. I wondered if there were palaces underneath the water and if we should find walls if we were brave enough to dive, an arch or, as some said, bells? The former gardens must be full of jellyfish and ribbonweed but nobody had seen the city and returned alive, except a fisher boy whose drunken master had upset their boat. Another coracle had picked up the child, with white hair and staring eyes, clasping a tiny stone cross.

"Suppose we went on," I asked, pointing to the line where the sea and sky seemed to touch, "should we come to another island?"

"If you sail far enough you come to the fog and the monsters. Some say that it is a belt that holds us from slipping off the edge of the world."

I tried to imagine the mist and what might be beyond it. It seemed strange to be willing to leave these love knots of golden weed floating on the tide and the friendly circle of the islands to probe some mysterious darkness and yet—the memory of a ragged storyteller danced on the waves below me—was it not the same feeling that had called Gawain from the fireside to the wet shingle of Belerion's beach? "Has no sailor been there?" I asked.

"A man was carried westwards in my grandfather's time. He drifted for two days in a cloud that almost stifled him, sometimes in silence, sometimes among scrunching noises or wails. There were no birds, he said, but a black head with two curved beaks reared itself beside the boat and would have capsized it had the fog not fallen again."

All the same I should like to try my luck or at least, I thought in sudden prudence, sail along the edge of whatever lay beyond the horizon. We were drawing close now to a couple of islets full of birds. "There she is!" Erbin shouted and I saw a dark mass wedged against the rocks. It looked at first as if the ship were anchored there but only a stump of the mast was left and the sea was pouring out of several holes in her stern with a grinding, terrifying roar. The waves raced forward like young wolves, leaping up in the air, falling on the bulwarks to tear them apart; there would soon be plenty of timber for the treeless islanders, but we could not approach the vessel because of a current that thundered between the main rocks and an outlying reef.

We were not the first to arrive. Twenty boats had already gathered into a circle around the wreck. We pulled into the shelter of one of the larger fishing vessels and a familiar voice shouted, "So you've come at last? Have you got anything to eat?"

I looked up, gaping. My uncle, in Dungarth's old

jacket that was much too small for him, was eating, yes, actually eating, a large piece of dried fish. It was the first time that I had ever seen him out of his robes. The sun had burnt his face during the last days, he was smiling and looked, to my astonishment, little different from the sailors surrounding him. "How did you get here?" I yelled.

"One of you boys might have told me what was happening. Dungarth fetched me and lent me some clothes. By the time I went into your hut, you had gone. If you had wakened me, you would have spared yourselves a long row. Rewards are not always to the hasty."

How characteristic of my uncle to turn everything into a moral tale! I clenched my fists but at that moment Honorius yelled "Catch" and Erbin grabbed a cloth so full of bread and meat that I had to forgive him.

"Where was the boat from?" Erbin shouted between mouthfuls.

"It's a Cornish ship, bound for Wales. She's too small for the Breton trade."

"Are there any survivors?" I asked curiously.

"No, they must have been washed away when she first struck."

"But we've found two good planks," Dungarth pointed to the timber that had been lashed together and was floating at the stern, "Over there they've got a cask but we don't know what's inside it."

"Water," Erbin answered promptly and everybody laughed.

After our headlong rush through the darkness, I was

disappointed to feel so little sense of disaster around me. Perhaps it was because the men lived so continuously with danger that they had learned to take it with a light heart. I tried to imagine the feelings of the crew as the ship had foundered and a great wave swept them over the side but the sun was up, the wind had blown the fog away and we seemed more like fishermen clustered about a shoal of pilchards than men watching a wreck. Now and again one of our number ventured forward to hook another piece of floating wood but it would have been madness to approach the actual rocks. We rolled up and down on the uneasy waves until I began to turn green. "Courage, it will be over in a few moments," Erbin teased; he had noticed the color of my face.

"Look!" Dungarth yelled, shading his eyes with his hand, "She's going."

There was a splintering of wood, we could feel if we could not see the rush of water through what was left of the ship and then, as the wave receded again, a black dot emerged, clinging to a fragment of the bow that was still wedged into a cleft.

"There's a seal on board," a voice behind me said in surprise.

"No," Dungarth answered, clutching a rope to steady himself, "it's a man."

A howl rather than a cry reached our ears from the white blob that we now recognized was a face. Another wave broke with full force over the wreckage while we gripped whatever was handy, waiting for the end. "He's still there!" Dungarth pointed in astonishment to the figure that was now crouching on a spar, preparing to dive. "If he would only jump into the deep water on the other side, we might reach him," Erbin said anxiously; the companionship that seafarers feel for one another in danger had wiped his feeling about strangers momentarily from his mind. "But how can we make him hear us?"

"The fool! He is going to plunge straight onto the rocks."

The man leaned forward but was either terrified by what he saw or unable to keep his balance on the edge of the slippery wood. A wave swept over him again but he emerged as it receded, clinging to a dangling rope. "The other side," Dungarth yelled, waving his arm. The sailor did not hear. He leaned forward as if he were about to slide directly into the surf. "Left!" The order rang out in the deep, commanding voice that Honorius used to make a proclamation or to end a ceremony, "Jump left."

"Quick." Erbin bent forward over his oar and we shot forward with another coracle from the end of the line. "Don't drown my nephew," Honorius shouted as we passed him.

"Better be drowned than go back to Lestowder," I muttered but the edge of the current caught us and I had not breath left to talk. The spray splashed into our faces and I thought as we mounted each wave that we should turn upside down. We were trying to dodge the current by sweeping round towards the back of the island, although there was little hope that the man could keep afloat until we reached him. "Do exactly as I tell you," Erbin ordered sternly, "if we capsize, we are men, not seals."

There was plenty of wreckage about us now and the other boat had to make a sudden turn to avoid being staved in by a splintered board. Erbin kept us skillfully out of the actual current but we rode up and down the walls of green water until I felt my arms would drop from their sockets. We heard a yell from the onlookers behind us and knew that the sailor had jumped but by this time I was so frightened that I kept my eyes fixed on Erbin's shoulders. I longed to go back but there could be no turning in such a sea. I wished I had not boasted; even Kaden at this moment seemed friendlier than the ocean. "I can see him," Erbin yelled. I ventured a quick glance but there was nothing but a length of oreweed torn off in the storm and a splinter from a plank. Something bobbed up to the top of the wave and vanished again. The two men in the other coracle pressed forward. A red, salt-stained ribbon drifted under my oar that one of the crew must have bought in some market place for his wife. "There he is." We swerved to the side and I saw a spar floating towards us with a black lump stretched along its length.

"Don't move," Erbin said anxiously, "keep the balance." The boat tipped as he leaned over and snatched at the man's coat but his fingers slid from the wet rags and the spar slid past. "Keep the balance," he yelled again, trying to grip the sailor's hair. The coracle rolled over dangerously although I was doing my best to keep it straight. "He's lashed himself to the wood," the fisher-man shouted from the other craft. He leaned over with a knife in his hand as they came abreast of us, we tipped again until I thought that we must go under, then some-thing wet and heavy landed almost on my feet, partly pulled by Erbin and partly shoved aboard by the other men. Slowly, very slowly, we regained our position and started to row back towards the waiting vessels. "They've left us the man and taken the timber," my com-panion grumbled. "Is the fellow even alive?" I could not stop rowing but the head rolled sideways as we struck another big sea and I gasped; until we reached the stern figure still standing at Dungarth's side, I—and I alone—knew that it was Lydd.

A fog settled over the islands, then it rained and it was impossible to walk from one hut to another without getting drenched to the knees in the long, feathery grass. It may have been the chilly air after the hot August days but a fever broke out in the village and Honorius was among its first victims. The leech was anxious; my uncle had weakened himself fasting beyond the limits of the days of mourning and it was now three days since I had been allowed to see him. I sat on a boulder, huddled in a cloak, with the future as indistinct as the sheep moving through the mist in front of me, wondering if my diso-bedience had helped to bring on the sickness?

"Come and warm yourself at our hut," a voice said mockingly, "you will get a fever yourself sitting out on those wet stones." I looked up to find Lydd, an old sack over his shoulders, standing at my side. "At least," he added triumphantly, "weather like this blots out the sea."

I could understand his aversion after his experiences on the wreck. We had hardly spoken to each other since we had landed. My uncle got him a lodging in the town and bought him some old clothes and Lydd had soon found work with a farmer, helping to mend a neglected wall.

"Come over to us," I suggested, "it's nearer." I shared a hut with Dungarth and the steersman.

"What would Honorius say?" he teased.

I hesitated: my uncle had forbidden me to talk to Lydd and I had actually forgotten about him during a couple of sunny days before the weather had broken when Erbin and I had gone mackerel fishing. "We shall be alone," I said, my curiosity reawakened, "the others have gone to the town and will not be back before night-fall."

"Your captain wants to sail as soon as this fog lifts. He says it is a sign that the autumn gales will begin sooner than usual."

"Are you coming with us?" I asked. I had not thought until this moment about Lydd's irregular position on the islands.

"Yes, they made me walk over to Peninnis and take some foolish oath before the salt water was out of my lungs. It was a waste af time although I could swear with an easy conscience never to lead a ship here. All I ask is to get safely back to the mainland."

"We cannot leave until my uncle is strong enough to say the final prayers."

"Your are nearer, no doubt, to the counsels of our uncle than I am," Lydd said with a scornful emphasis upon the word *our,* "but the sooner he returns to Cornwall the better. They were saying at Peninnis, though I don't know how they heard the story, that the King is going to dismiss his father's priests and take their land."

"Perhaps the seer had a dream."

"Or saw a signal from the cliffs. The rumor of a man's fall spreads more rapidly than his rise. Anyhow, they are alarmed. The islanders will suffer if there are no more burials and no tributes of corn."

"But, Lydd, they might starve." I had been too full of my own problems to realize that a change of rulers could also harm the islands. "Erbin told me that once the grain ship was wrecked, long ago, and most of the children died during the next winter because they had only seaweed and a little pulse to eat with their fish."

"What does Honorius think?"

"He tells me nothing, you forgot I am in disgrace." I knew that he would have heard about my escapade from one of the sailors.

"You went to the fair to see your kinsmen. What a crime!" Lydd laughed and I thought that if he would only comb his hair and wash his face occasionally he would be a handsome fellow with his long runner's legs. He seemed to take a pride in wearing torn clothes, there was already a rent from the elbow to the wrist in the leather jacket that my uncle had purchased for him, and yet, as he looked at me suddenly with an almost pleading expression on his face, I felt that he was only asking me for friendliness.

"If I could once make him understand . . ." The fog was beginning to lift and a cold, gray sea flecked here and there with white beat steadily over the rocks. "I was born to be a sailor and not to chant staves."

"I could have been a son to him as well if he had bound me to some merchant," Lydd flopped down on the boulder beside me in spite of its being wet, "and useful as well because I could have kept him in touch with the villages. Things have changed so much during the last years. You know, the people say that if they follow the Christians they can cut down more trees."

I had heard them grumble during my last summer at Godrevy. Nobody wanted to touch the big oaks but the swineherds complained that most of the patches of forest behind our wind-swept coast were sacred to the priests and that they had nowhere to drive their pigs at acorn time. "Honorius would not listen to us," I said and wondered if this were obstinacy in him or courage?

"You remind me, Ruan, of the child I once was. I have friends in Wales and I still want to join them. Come and spend the winter with me there. You are too young at present to know your own mind."

"I can pull a coracle as strongly as Erbin."

"Boy's talk. I have no doubt that you are as strong as a young bull but you are rooted to your village and it would be a pity to return to Lestowder and regret it for the rest of your life. If you really want to be a sailor, there will be plenty of ships looking for a crew next spring; otherwise, if you prefer to be a wealthy uncle's nephew I can help you get to Cornwall again. Have no fear, you are his favorite, he would soon forgive you."

"I cannot leave him if he is in danger."

"The King will not harm him, he will not want to upset the start of his reign. At worst, he will make him give up some of his land."

"Honorius has never used wealth for himself."

"I know, a cup of water and a cake of meal." Lydd wrinkled his nose up in a grimace. "He would not even spare a little silver to buy me a share in a trading venture. I was alone, Ruan, when I ran away. You have a friend. All you have to do is to trust me."

The rain had stopped and I felt suddenly as if a part of me were light enough to join the gulls in their freedom overhead. Then I remembered how my courage failed whenever I was in my uncle's presence. "But he would not let me go," I moaned.

"Leave it to me. Even Honorius will need a night's sleep after we land before riding to Lestowder. If I can find a ship bound for Wales I will come for you."

"I do not want to go to Wales, I want to stay here."

"They would find some means to send you to your uncle. If the corn ship does not leave next summer, I heard Dungarth promise that he would bring over a cargo in his kinsman's vessel. Prove your independence and he will bring you back with him."

"I must think it over," I said wearily, balancing my uncle's need and the islands against each other.

78

"It was lonely the first night," Lydd put his hand upon my shoulder, "I slept in the bracken and stirred at every noise. Afterwards I found a master and went with him as far as Bodmin. Every day seemed happier than the last because I was a man and not my uncle's half-acknowledged ward."

"I know it was hard." For a moment something under the grimy clothes and the rough voice drew me nearer to Lydd than I was even to Erbin. "I will come," I said boldly, "if you can find a ship."

"Leave it to me," Lydd jumped to his feet, "in spite of what you said about Dungarth being away, he is coming up the hill at this moment with the leech and it is better that he does not see us together. Farewell but trust me, I may not see you alone again before we land." He slipped away before I could answer and to steady my thoughts, that were beating like two currents meeting each other in a swirl of water, I walked rapidly down towards my friends.

The hours passed as slowly as the steps of the genealogies but on the fourth day the fog thinned out towards sunset and the leech summoned me. "Your uncle wishes to speak with you," he said, "do not stay long. He is weak and the fever has not entirely left him."

The inside of the hut smelt of sickness and bitter herbs. They had spread a double layer of rushes under the pallet and I stopped abruptly at the threshold; the face that looked up at me was the color of dried bone. "Take the stool," Honorius said feebly, "I have much to say and so little time."

"How is your chest?" I faltered, wondering how a man could change so much in four days.

"I shall live," my uncle answered quietly, "I know this although I am not a seer. Do not look frightened, nephew, once you take office you will have to accustom yourself to sickness and death."

I did not answer; it flashed across my mind that it was unfair to remind me of my destiny at such a moment and then was ashamed of the thought while Honorius was so ill.

"Yes, Ruan, I shall return to Cornwall but not to serve this King as I served his father. Believe me, nephew, you must learn from Kaden all that he can teach you, we have not many months left."

"You will get well," I lied, "the leech told me that your strength would come back to you in another few days."

"Perhaps." Honorius coughed a little and closed his eyes. I thought that he was falling asleep but he opened them again after a few moments and smiled at me. "Listen, Ruan, I loved learning as much as you love a ship and Tudwal, my master, who held this office until I succeeded him, sent me to study in Gaul. I must have been about your age."

"How long were you away?" It was out of fashion now for our rulers to leave the kingdom and although I knew that my uncle had made a voyage in his youth he had seldom spoken about it to his pupils.

"Three years. It was the happiest time of my life. The winters in Brittany are colder than they are with us but the summers are warm and dry. I was fortunate because the barbarians had driven the father of my teacher, Melus, out of Wales so the family spoke our tongue." He coughed again and I offered him a cup that the leech had left on top of another stool. "It's feverfew mixed with camomile," Honorius muttered with a grimace. "I would rather have water."

I stuck another stick or two upon the fire. If the sky cleared Erbin would take me fishing in the morning and we would land and cook our mackerel on some isle. My uncle was watching me, I noticed, so I came back and sat down again beside him.

"I learned to read and Melus taught me rhetoric; believe me, Ruan, the building up of a whole, point by point, can be as fascinating to some minds as swordplay. The foundation stone of any kingdom is law and unless we follow our traditions, harsh though some of them may seem, what is the end but anarchy, with the better-armed man seizing his neighbor's land? Melus hoped that our teachings would transform the conquerors but I was doubtful; when men make compromises, it is always the stronger mind that wins. I did not tell him what I felt because he was poor and it was kinder to let him dream of a day when he might regain his grandfather's farm. Our harbor was a sheltered place." It might be still the fever but my uncle's eyes shone as I had never seen them shine during his prayers. "We were cut off from the rest of Gaul by a forest and I knew better than Melus, I think, how those trees protected us. Men are like wolves, plunder means more to them than prayers, but there were no roads and plenty of wild beasts so they left us alone. Yet like you, Ruan, I was discontented, I wanted to become some scholar's servant and take ship with him to the South."

"Oh, why didn't you!" I said involuntarily. How much happier we should both have been if this had happened.

"Melus was not opposed to the idea. There was said to be a philosopher at Massilia who was trying to reconcile some of the new ideas that were floating about the world with our traditions. We talked about my journey the whole of one winter round the fire. Then spring came and later, just as they were about to cut the hay, a Cornish ship entered the harbor. Its captain brought a message to me from Tudwal: he was getting old and wanted me to return."

"You should have gone to Massilia," I said.

"I thought so at that moment. I hated Tudwal as you, Ruan, hate me now. I left Melus and my friends and walked for a couple of hours along a valley that I knew to an orchard full of neglected apple trees. Its owner had abandoned it, he was afraid of working alone so far from the town. I sat on a flat stone that had toppled out of the wall, running my fingers along the mosses growing in the cracks and arguing that, though I owed my master loyalty, if I studied the new philosophy my knowledge might help every human being in Lestowder on my return. It was almost sunset before Melus found me. One of those summer rains had started and we got wet through as we fought the matter out, walking home. You know, Ruan, it was my fever but I felt that he was sitting here beside me with the raindrops glistening in his old cap, the first night that I was ill. I certainly heard his words again, ringing in my ears. 'Knowledge comes in stages, friend; if we learn too much we lose touch with the folk about us and then it is harder to help them. Accept your duty and life will gradually grow easier.' "

"And did it?" I asked.

"I will not lie to you, Ruan; no, not for a long time."

I suspected from the expression on my uncle's face that he was seeing not the wattles of the hut but a wilder and stranger landscape. "I think you should have gone to Massilia," I said again, wondering why he should want me to repeat his own experience after he had suffered so much in his youth?

"I knew when I said goodbye to Melus afterwards that I should never see him again, never have another friend." A shiver ran down my back at these words. Should I be separated from Erbin always after we sailed?

The pallet was crooked, some of the rushes were scattered over the floor, the wood was damp and the fire smoking so much that I began to cough myself. My uncle drank some more of the liquid in the cup and continued slowly, as if he were thinking over every word, "If the King dismisses me," his fingers gripped the chain that because of his sickness was lying next him on the stool, "I shall still stay with the people till I die. Perhaps your brother will spare me a corner by the fire or if he is afraid, Kaden, I know, will remain with me. It will be time enough then, Ruan, to decide about your future. At present, I expect you to be obedient."

"We could sail together to Massilia," I suggested, "perhaps your philosopher is still alive?" Honorius could study while I wandered about the city, looking for craftsmen who made the decorated bowls like the one that I had seen at the fair.

"It is too late. After all these years I am not going to neglect my duty at the finish. I do not want to leave you unprotected, Ruan, you are young and gave up your share of your inheritance when you became my pupil. Open that chest over there by the wall."

It took me a few moments to lift the lid; the wood had swollen in the damp air. At first I could see only the robe that Honorius had worn on the day of the funeral; there was a mark on the hem where a burning cinder had scorched it. "Put your hand down the side until you feel a small bag," my uncle commanded but there seemed to be nothing but the folds of his summer cloak. "Can't you find it?" he asked anxiously. "You had better spread the things one by one on the floor."

I glanced down at the dirty rushes where somebody had spilt a bowl of soup and ran my arm round the edge again. This time I felt a piece of soft hide under my finger tips and lifted out a small but surprisingly heavy wallet. "Bring it to me here," my uncle ordered. He tried to untie the strings but the effort was too much for him. "Look inside it yourself," he said feebly and I took out seven links of heavy Irish gold.

"This was a free gift from the King I served," Honorius said. "Put five links in the wallet and wear it always round your neck. Tie the other two up in a cloth

84

and put them back in the chest. I am not giving you the gold to use now but a day may come when you may need it. No, Ruan, it is useless arguing with me, you will not shake my will."

"Let me stay here." I thought of Erbin racing towards a silver pool at dawn with a shell's span of sunlight dazzling us between gray clouds. "I will even go to Peninnis if I must but let me stay here."

"And leave me?"

I do not know what I should have answered but the leech came in at that moment, followed by a woman with a bowl of soup. "He is better," he said in a low voice after he had felt my uncle's forehead, "but these long fasts must stop. He has been much weakened by this sickness."

"You can go, Ruan." Honorius looked at me steadily from his pallet and the old authority seemed to have come back into his voice. "I shall be strong enough to make the final offerings in another three days and afterwards the sooner we return to Cornwall the better. You can tell Dungarth from me to begin preparing the ship."

It was the harvest moon. I thought of our hives in the orchard at Godrevy as I looked up at the stars and of a swarm of bees that I had once seen in the cleft of an old tree. This was my last night of freedom and I knew that if they took me to Lestowder I should die; not in body, alas, but in spirit. Kaden had been waiting for us at the quay when we had landed. My resolution to protect my uncle had faded as soon as I had smelt the schoolyard dust about his clothes and seen his thin, hard mouth. Honorius had noticed my despair. "You may stay the night with your kinsman provided you join me at sunrise," he had said in his kindest voice, disregarding Kaden's signs. "If we leave as soon as it is light we shall reach home before it is dusk."

I wanted now to make my lost childhood rise and shield me but trying for something so impossible merely broke the immediate sense of darkness, ripening apples and the smell of drying nets. I was about to bang my head against the wall to drive what thoughts I had out of my stupid head when I heard a voice whispering at my elbow, "Well, Ruan, have you made up your mind? There is a ship sailing tomorrow to Wales."

I turned at once and said aloud in my excitement, "Will the captain take me?"

"Careful," Lydd scolded, a finger at his lips, "do you want to bring Dungarth out looking for gossiping strangers? We can work through the winter on my comrade's farm."

"But I shall lose Godrevy," I answered though without much conviction. "It is almost the same as becoming an outlaw."

"You cannot have everything you want, Ruan; besides, if you are unhappy there is sure to be a boat returning here in the spring."

"And my uncle? And the King?"

"Whatever the prince thought while his father was alive, he is too shrewd to upset the people now until he is crowned and sure of his power. Nothing is going to happen to that uncle of ours before next summer and if you want to go back to him both of you can say that you went to Wales to study their traditions."

It was true. One of my fellow pupils was the nephew of a Welsh priest who had come to us for a year to learn the Cornish genealogies. A dog barked in the distance, there was salt in the air and I knew that I had to take the chance that destiny was offering me or die. "How did you get in," I asked, "up the wall and down the old tree?"

"Wait a moment, Ruan, we shall have to pay some passage money. Have you any silver?"

The gold pieces hung heavily round my neck. They still belonged to my uncle but in my present need if Lydd had known that they were there and had asked for them I believe that I should have handed him the wallet. I untied instead the bag that I wore at my belt and poured the contents into my hand: there was one silver link and a few small coins.

Lydd looked at the heap in disappointment. "His favorite nephew and you have less to show for it than a shepherd boy."

"We could work our way."

"I'm no sailor, Ruan, and all I had was forfeit to the sea."

I remembered the crash of the waves as Lydd looked at me reproachfully and the body that had tumbled towards us like a black, drowning seal. He was braver than I was to risk another voyage at once so late in the year, simply to join his friend. "Erbin gave me a ring," I said reluctantly, "but it was a token of his friendship and I want to keep it."

"Show it me."

I took it from under the collar of my coat where I had hidden it in case my uncle asked for it. It was an old piece of heavy silver.

"Your friend will understand because this is your way back to him. Once you are in Kaden's hands, there will be no more seafaring. But you must choose."

My ears caught the low, quiet murmur of the surge along the shore. After they brought the ponies here at dawn it would be too late, not for a season only but for life, and I pressed the ring into Lydd's hand without another word.

"Can you fetch your cloak without being noticed?"

I nodded and stepped inside the low doorway. Dungarth was still talking to his wife about a wattle fence that would have to be repaired. How strange it was that he should spend his first hours at home grumbling about the cost of stakes after all the mystery and adventure of the islands! The blazing pyre came back to me and the rush over the tumbling, green waves towards the wreck. My bundle was still lying where I had left it at the foot of the whitewashed wall. I picked it up and was stealing softly out again when I kicked a small stool over in the darkness. "What are you doing, Ruan?" Dungarth asked in a startled voice. "I thought you were asleep this last hour."

"There is no air in the house after being aboard a ship. I was taking my sleeping fleece out to the garden."

"Not under the moon!" I heard the swish of his wife's

skirt against the bench as she stood up. "You'll lose your wits if you sleep in the moonlight."

I trembled. Had I lost my chance through a bit of foolish carelessness or was it a sign that I must not leave my uncle? My fingers dug into the rough canvas of my pack until the captain growled reassuringly, "Oh, let the boy sleep where he will tonight so long as he is quiet and does not wake the neighbors."

Lydd had gone but after a moment's search I found him waiting for me by the withered tree that Dungarth was always going to cut down when he had the time but that still stood at the end of the garden. "You fool," he said, seizing me by the sleeve, "can't you walk five paces in the dark without making noise enough to rouse every dog in the street? I almost left you to the mercy of Kaden's rod."

We scrambled onto a bough and this time I took good care neither to snap a twig nor to let my belt buckle rasp against the top stone of the wall. Lydd let himself down lightly and I followed, there was nobody in sight and we trotted along the narrow pathway and round another house until we came down to the beach.

The moonlight shone on a mass of empty limpet shells, there was a strong stench of seaweed and as we scrunched across the small pebbles and the sticky sand I thought with surprise that this was almost the identical landscape that the harper had described when he was telling us about Gawain's last journey. There was even a sailor waiting beside a coracle drawn partly up the beach. He greeted Lydd as if they were old friends.

"You go first, Ruan, I have to fetch my cloak."

I hesitated; it would be a strange vessel where nobody knew me and where they might laugh at me for my lack of skill. Lydd was my last link with a familiar life. "Let me wait for you here," I pleaded.

"I can't take you both at once," the sailor said, smiling at my companion.

"There is nothing to fear, Ruan, we must not let the captain see us until we have sailed, so the sooner you go aboard the quicker I can join you." Lydd stooped forward and helped shove the coracle gently into the sea.

"It's an old scow," the sailor said, handing me a broken jar, "you bale, I'll row." I could feel the water splashing around my shoes (neither Dungarth nor Erbin would have allowed such a craft to be used until it had been mended) so it was not until I had emptied a score of potfuls over the side that I ventured to look up again. All I could see was Lydd scrambling over the stones at the top of the beach and the black hull of my new ship rising suddenly to the right of us.

It was broad daylight when I woke after an uneasy feeling of suffocation. The sailor had hidden me behind a roll of sailcloth; a flap of it was loose and covering my mouth. I was being flung as well against a hard piece of timber as the ship rolled but the more I tried to free myself the more firmly I got the cloth entangled round my head. We slithered towards the opposite side and it loosened a little, "Help!" I yelled in terror, "help!"

"It's not a pig," somebody joked, "it's a boy."

Two sailors, dripping with water because we had just

shipped a heavy sea, dragged the obstacles away and hauled me to my feet. I took a deep breath of fresh air and looked at the coast. We were off the great cliff that marked the end of Dumnonia and the seas were breaking in great white manes of spray over the rocks. The wind was favorable, our oars were shipped and the still strong September sun turned the surf into dazzling lights. I stood there, clutching my bundle that I had used as a pillow, till a man strode up to me. I knew from his silver arm-band and the lynx-fur cap on his head that he must be the captain. "How did you get aboard?" he asked.

"My companion paid for our passages, he is here too," I answered anxiously. Suppose Lydd had hidden himself behind a cask where there was no rope that he could grip and he had been washed overboard? It was my fault, I had encouraged him to tempt the sea again instead of accepting my uncle's offer.

"Nobody spoke to me about a passage. If the wind had not got up so that we sailed at dawn suddenly, the sail-cloth would have been stowed in its proper place, we should have found you and tossed you into the harbor to swim ashore. Why are you here? You will only make it worse if you tell me lies."

"I gave my friend a ring to pay for us both as far as Wales. The man who brought me aboard last night knew him and is one of your crew."

"Name him then, we are all here." I looked slowly from one weather-beaten face to the other and realized with horror that they were all unknown to me. I was away from my own folk for the first time in my life and in the middle of strangers. "But . . ." I gasped, "it was somebody else."

I think that the captain must have seen from the utter look of astonishment on my face that I was speaking the truth. "Did you meet him in a tavern?" he asked.

An old fellow with graying hair and a knife in his hands spat over the side, looked me up and down and said slowly, "I was having my pot of ale at Mother Elen's last night, it's the only place left where they do not mix the drink with well water, but as you know, her father was . . ."

"Yes, yes," the captain said impatiently, "we all know she should be mistress of Morva farm if she had her rights."

"And her husband was drowned not a league from where we are now . . ."

"In a fog, on a dark night," another sailor muttered.

"But what has Mother Elen got to do with this boy here?" The captain took off his cap, dusted it with his sleeve and put it back on his head again. "Was he there?"

"No, no, I didn't see him but it's a smoky place and I was sitting away from the door. I had had my sip of ale and a crust of bread to go with it, you young fellows gulp your drink and then wonder why you pant like a dog before a thunderstorm, heaving up the anchor the next morning. Now . . ."

"What has all this got to do with the boy?" the captain grumbled. "We have got to reef the sail as soon as we round the point."

"A man sat down beside me and I told him to watch the stool, there was a crack in one of the legs and I knew a farmer . . ."

"The boy, the boy!"

"You are always in a hurry but it won't get you any further in the end. Well, this man, if you want to know, asked me where we were bound. He said he had a young cousin who had got himself into trouble over a girl and he wanted to find a ship for him. He had a slit in his coat from the elbow to the wrist."

"And thick, black hair?"

"Yes," the old man spat again and grinned at me maliciously.

"I was in no trouble," I said angrily, "Lydd and I were going to Wales to make our fortunes together. And . . . I remember now . . . the man who brought me to this ship had a wart on his cheek."

"Old Fishbones! He would do anything for ale except work."

"The man with the slit coat said that he was riding to Bodmin with a peddler. He wanted to get away from the sight of the sea."

"He took my ring!" I shouted and if we had been near enough to the coast I believe that I should have dived over the side and gone in search of him. The men roared with laughter as they saw me clench my fists and the captain said with a flicker of curiosity, "Had you known the fellow long?"

"All my life. The only true part of his story was that we were kinsmen of a sort."

93

"There's a bad streak somewhere in every family. I could thrash you but I believe you are speaking the truth when you say you have been robbed. Here, someone, give him a broom, he can help wash down the deck," the captain smiled at me in quite a friendly manner and added, "Hard work, boy, is as good a salve for anger as anything I know."

I took the handle that they thrust into my hands. At this very moment, no doubt, Lydd was riding over the moors on a pony bought with the ring that I had given him so trustingly, and whistling gaily when he thought of the trick he had played on Honorius again. I ought to have told myself that my present fate was the reward of my own falseness but this was too strong a word. I had told my uncle over and over that if he caged me again, I should die. Yes, even at this moment of loneliness and uncertainty I was glad to be standing on the rolling ship and not in front of Kaden in our courtyard. I looked round, there were no other ships near us but suddenly, and it brought my circumstances home to me more than any of the jests that the sailors shouted in passing, I saw a few silver points far off on the horizon. The islands were there, Erbin, the Sound that I loved and I wondered now if I should ever see them again? "Sweep, boy," somebody shouted angrily, "we've no room for passengers," and a wave broke that moment over the side, drenching me to the skin and sending us all sliding into the scuppers.

# II

HIS was a soft landscape, green and gray, a Cornwall dipped in water. It had neither the hardness of my native cliffs nor the remoteness of the Scillys. Now it seemed almost home; this was the second time that we had come to winter here and though the gales might thunder above our low huts, in southern Ireland there was unlikely to be much snow.

It was later in the season than we usually landed but an irritating number of small repairs had held us in Wales, fortunately because we had thus escaped a storm that had taken its toll of the northern fleet, returning to winter in its homeland. "This is the happiest day of the year," our steersman had just said, letting the still dry sand trickle between his toes. "The raiding season is over, we are safe in harbor with five months' sleep ahead of us and we have even some pieces of silver."

I shifted my gear from one shoulder to the other because I was more used to oars at present than to struggling across a marshy plain where the mud dragged my feet down at every step, but the air was mild, I was alone and free to follow my own will for the first time in many weeks. Osmund, our captain, knowing that I spoke a little of the language, had sent me ahead to find a shelter for himself and the crew.

I suppose I had been walking for about an hour before I came to the track that led up from the bog. It was not a path that the villagers often used but one that we had discovered during the previous spring when we had begun to prepare our *Seagull* for her voyage. It seemed to have been deserted while we had been away because grass was growing in the ruts again and a bare patch, where we had left the water casks one afternoon, was already thick with thistles. The roar of the waves over the great, sweeping sands lessened as I climbed, the sun was out, the last tiny, golden buds crept up the furze bushes. "The happiest day in the year"? Yes, so it was for most sailors but thankful as I was to feel the ground under my feet this was the ending of the season; the cold would come, and with it how much boasting and drunkenness around the peat fires? We should be lucky if we did not lose more than one of the men in some stupid brawl before the next muster. My longing to wander was as great as ever but five years at sea had blunted some of my enthusiasm. It might have been the short, lulling motion of the wind through the gorse but I kept thinking of Honorius as I climbed. He had always liked the last blossoms of the year. A sailor whom I had once met when we were filling up our water casks had told me that my uncle had died at my brother's farm, shortly after my flight. I could have made no other choice, I knew, yet I wished that he had given me his blessing; then perhaps I could have found a way out from the moodiness that was still my chief enemy and accepted life as easily as my shipmates. Yet April would flash by with the speed of a doe through the thickets, we should sing as we launched our boat again and another round of watches, fears and quarrels would begin, so similar in pattern every season that the only difference between the first voyage of a father and of his son was the twenty years in age between them. What was the purpose of it all? I did not want to be a farmer, bound to a furrow of land, nor a smith, tied to his forge, but the earth covered itself with water mint and sweet-smelling herbs, the waves stole up the shingle, each having its task, whereas man, man . . .

"Still alive, Ruan? Or have you turned herdsman after all?"

I looked up in utter surprise, annoyed that I had been too absorbed by my own speculations to walk with my customary prudence. I did not recognize the face at first, then as the grin widened under a tangled crop of hair I recognized the speaker in spite of the lapse of time.

"Why, Lydd!" I exclaimed, "how did you get here? But I'm still a sailor. I'm Osmund the Pilot's man."

"The Pilot! The Fog-smeller, you mean," and Lydd laughed. It was said of Osmund that he preferred a sober job of carrying cargo to raiding the coast and that he cared for his ship as if she had been a maid. I had remained with him for three years precisely because I admired both qualities. "We did well enough this voyage," I boasted and then was angry that I had allowed Lydd to provoke such an answer before I had bargained for our winter quarters. "You played a nice trick on me," I added sharply, "you took my silver and sent me off to Wales where I had no friends."

"You know you were meant to be a sailor, Ruan, and by leaving our uncle you saved his life."

"I do not understand what you mean," I answered haughtily. The memory of my first winter, working for a household in Wales, was still as bitter as the taste of a withered dandelion chewed in a wayfarer's mouth.

"Your uncle asked Dungarth to search for you but he rode to Lestowder. The King sent for him and listened in complete silence, so they say, to the account of his father's burial. Then he put a heavy gold chain into your uncle's hands. Honorius understood. He asked permission to retire to your brother's farm on account of his age. He died there, but peacefully and on his own pallet, the following winter. As soon as he had left the Court, the King and all his followers were baptized."

"I ought to have been with him. It would have been little enough to sacrifice, those few short months."

"The King was told that you stayed behind on the islands. He could afford to be merciful to an old and dying man whom the people loved but if a youth had been there to rally them round him and fight for his inheritance it would have been a different matter." Lydd tapped the handle of his dagger with another grin.

If the story were true, I had probably saved my uncle from a savage death, though if he were aware of this (and luckily I thought that this was doubtful) it would only have increased his condemnation of my disobedience. According to him, I had betrayed our tradition and he probably ascribed his dismissal, at least in part, to his failure to hold me from what he had called "the world."

"What happened to Kaden and the other pupils?" I asked, curiosity getting the better of my anger.

"Most of them moved quietly over to the new priest's chapel but Kaden took a couple of the boys to a valley in Wales where one of them had lived. They say that the King was so pleased to disperse them without trouble that he gave them six silver links as journey money."

"And my brother?"

"Oh, as soon as your uncle was dead and he had spent what was left of the chain on buying new cattle he was baptized as well. He's a prudent man and taking no chances; the last time that I walked across his wood, it must be two years ago, there was still a garland hanging from the oak."

"Whatever made you leave Cornwall?" I noticed that Lydd had lost two of his teeth and that there was a silver badge on his tattered coat.

"I got into a bit of trouble at Bodmin Fair. The traders manage such deals without any difficulty but I was alone and the watch came after me. I came across here to help a merchant with his bales but I liked the place and now I'm one of Moram's men," he mentioned the chief who ruled this stretch of coast, "he is generous but poor. Too many of his subjects join your crews."

"We have no Irishmen aboard." I wondered if Lydd had tricked me just to save my uncle's life or if he had wanted to destroy my chances because he had lost his own?

"You know your way," he continued. "Strangers generally turn to the right at the two birches and find themselves floundering in the mud again a little further on."

"We were here last winter."

"It's a good climate," Lydd grinned as he scratched an ear. "Moram thinks that the Christians drove me out, he doesn't like them. I can tell him the same story about yourself; if he likes a man, he is a good master."

I shook my head. I had no wish to accept a favor from Lydd nor even to stay with him in the same village. "I'm pledged to Osmund," I said, "and unlike you, although I have only just landed, I miss the sea."

"So young!" Lydd clapped me on the shoulder as if he had been my elder brother. "Let me come and help you at the village. I speak their tongue now as easily as Cornish."

"Thanks, but I am only walking over to see a friend and get my legs used to solid ground again. Osmund has not decided yet where he wants to settle."

"Tell him to keep away from the beach, the huts there are damp in winter." Lydd looked up at the sky and the thought flashed across my mind that in spite of his boasts he was afraid of returning late to his master's hall. "I can't linger now," he said, "but come and see me once your oars are stowed away. And don't forget, if your captain wants a bargain in dried meat or a puppy to amuse him while he is ashore, I'm his man. The people here are thieves but for your sake I shall treat him like a brother and see that they make him a fair price. It is less than three hours to Moram's hall but be sure to take a guide. His guards find hunting strangers as good a pastime as hunting hares. They know me and I have my badge," he tapped the brooch that gleamed so strangely on his ragged coat, "but get a village boy to bring you out. We have much to talk about after all these years." He smiled as if we were cousins at least.

I nodded gravely and as he raced across the pasture at a tremendous pace I remembered how he had beaten all the runners at Godrevy during my childhood. He slackened his stride to scramble up and over a low bank and as he got to the top of it he turned and waved. I waved back and, full of a strange uneasiness, continued on my way. Perhaps I had misjudged the fellow, nobody could have seemed more friendly, yet how could a few cheerful words obliterate the knocks, curses and loneliness of that first year away from home? I had little enough to show for five voyages. It was only during the last one that Osmund had tried me out as second steersman after a man had had his arm crippled by the blow of a spar and due then less to my skill than because I could speak a smattering of several languages and was useful to him in port. They were burning the summer's rubbish in a field as I reached the first hut of the village to which I was bound. Perhaps the anxiety that I felt came as much from the change of season as from my meeting with Lydd? I wiped my shoes on a tuft of grass, brushed away some thistledown from my sleeve and asked a boy if the headman were at his house or in the meadows. After all, both of us had our separate tasks and it was unlikely that Lydd and I would often meet unless I asked permission to visit him at Moram's hall.

It was not a cold winter but I suffered in body and mind from the gray, wet days. Something inside me was stagnant and lazy while an undercurrent of restlessness drove me to ramble over the fields when I could have sprawled in front of a turf fire beside my comrades. I was weary of their stories and knew that if I heard Alfgar tell us again about the three-legged wolf that he had caught in a trap, my irritation would be so great that we should take to our weapons and the crew would be a man short in the spring. Yet I never hunted unless it were my turn nor checked the oars until Osmund sent me to the shed. "Ah," they were gossiping again though the smoke was so thick that I could not see their features, "once a man turns homeward with a single hare, saying that the wind has struck him in the small of the back, it's a sign he is growing old." Was this what was happening to me? I still looked at my arms to excuse myself for this or the other failure by whispering "When I come to my full strength" but I had recently caught sight of my face in a still unfrozen pool and I knew that my moment of maturity had come, and would, in a season or two, decline. "His force grew with the sun and waned with the moon." Where had I heard that proverb? In a story? Round a fire some other winter? Somebody poked the ashes and I coughed; then I saw, in a flash of memory, a harper's lean face above the crowd at Lestowder. It was raining but I sprang up and pushed my way through the skins at the door. I want to go home, I thought, home, but the village that I meant existed no longer. The ash may come from apple wood but who thinks of the tree or its fruit when he is raking out the fire?

There were few old men among us sailors; the risks were too great. Occasionally a voyage was lucky and a comrade would hoard his silver pieces until he could buy a few acres of land. A season or two later, he would usually return to beg for a place in the crew, when it was time to launch the ships. It was strange but such men, once they were sailors again, usually died the same year. Osmund said that their desertion had angered the gods or perhaps they had lost the sense of moving with the waves that came from months on the rowing benches. Anyhow, they fell overboard, caught a fever or were clumsy with their shields. "We live by the favor of the sea and we are its children as much as these gulls," Osmund would shout each May. "Life is short and hard but there is none of your pacing out of furrows, an hour up and an hour down, with nothing to look forward to when your teeth are worn but a saucer of scraps on a heap of scratchy heather."

I climbed a sloping down behind the village that led upwards to a small wood. We followed the spring and harvest processions to the oak at its center but otherwise the Irish never entered it and I was afraid myself to go inside the grove. I had found a hole, however, on the inner, wind-sheltered side of a bank at the edge of the boundary and had stuffed this with dry leaves and a little straw. I spent my leisure there, dreaming foolishly about the past, as if by merely thinking of it I could bring my boyhood back to me.

I crawled into the burrow now in spite of the mist. How different life would have been had Honorius not taken me away from my home! This was the way that I always began as if I were repeating an opening, ritual prayer. Up and down, down and up, like the seas that I often cursed and sometimes missed, memories rocked me into a chilly, prickling doze beneath my cloak and the rustling grasses.

It was my uncle who came first and most frequently into my thoughts, always with a sense of guilt. If only I could have made him understand me! I did not trust Lydd but I felt that this time his story was true because the Cornish sailor, who had no reason to lie, had said that Honorius had died at my brother's farm. Yet had my flight saved him or ought I, somehow, to have gone to Godrevy and stayed with him until the end? My anger over his dismissal might have brought disaster upon us all but reason is no match for conscience and I tossed disconsolately from side to side, wishing that he had put me directly into Dungarth's care or that I was sitting beside my mother again, while she dipped a wooden spoon into the pot hanging over the hearth, to pick out the bit of meat that I most liked.

I suppose that I had been in my refuge for a couple of hours, lost in the sloth of all the woodland creatures during the dead season, while the wind tore last year's nests out of the branches. How full the days seemed with disquiet and weariness. Was there no other pattern than a war cry or an unexpected shoal, the boasting that followed an occasional feast? If anything were constant, it was the sea; that and a tormenting wish, it was like hunger, to strip complexities away and find a truth beneath the surface of this confusing world. Yet where was the knowledge that I sought? "Ask!" framed itself in runic strokes across my mind, as if some tale were reflecting itself there in the sleepy, distant way that the waves move at low tide. The raindrops trickled through a crevice onto my face, the straw was too sparse to cover me properly and I turned over and over in deep melancholy upon my pallet of yellow leaves.

Ask! Ask what? I still did not know. Honorius, for all his wisdom, excluded happiness, those few moments that dissolved into some other sense, often near but seldom within reach. The words had been used too often, we heard them without response. Osmund was a leader, busy with immediate events. "A cloud, Ruan, is a cloud. It will not make my navigation easier if you call it a sheep." (Yet that day a flock of white, fleecy beasts had rambled across the sky.) What had I done myself but drift? I had never tried to find Dungarth although, for all I knew, the King might have ended the isolation of the islands. I could not explain my hesitation, nothing was clear, whatever I remembered seemed blotted out by a thicker fog than was ever met at sea. I turned again in the burrow, the sun was setting in a feather of gold along the western sky but like Gawain I did not know the question and again like Gawain, in a torrent of bewilderment, I fell asleep.

It was almost dark when I woke up and scrambled out of the burrow. I was angry with myself for being late because it was dangerous to be outside the village enclosure at nightfall. I stayed only long enough to push the straw back into position and spread a bough or two over it before starting to run towards the huts while a little light remained. It was a calm evening and as I crossed the stream I could just see the curious pattern that the flowing water made under a transparent skin of ice. I had almost reached the wattle fence when torches appeared on the opposite hill and I slackened my pace. What a fool I was! It was still another sign of this heavy winter sleepiness. I had forgotten that this was the last night of the year and that Osmund had invited men from many different districts to eat with us. If my companions missed me, they would suppose that I had gone to meet a friend. I could hear from the barking and whining that the dogs had been tied up to stakes and not left loose to warn us of intruders as was customary in the evening.

The sky was now black and pointed with stars. At another time I should have seen that it was beautiful and been thankful to have the heavy, clinging turf under my shoes instead of a heaving deck but I could not rid myself of the feeling that with all these miles of earth and sky around me I was in some prison. No memory evoked more than another shadow, I was like a child wailing for a trifle whose voice falters suddenly because it has forgotten the object for which it was crying. Nothing was sharp, the air itself was unnaturally sticky and warm, the offal pit on my left stank and if I had dared I should have gone straight to my rushes and slept on them till morning.

I lifted the hide carefully and entered our hut. My comrades had gone and the fire had been allowed to die down into embers. A figure stirred in the shadows; I recognized an old woman who sometimes cooked for us and who had been left, no doubt, to see that it was still burning on our return. "How late!" she grinned at me, "and how wet!" It was easy to see from the expression on her face that she supposed that I had been sleeping with some girl. I shook her hand impatiently away (she was squeezing the moisture from my cloak between her dirty fingers) and answered shortly, "I went to look for my captain's hound, it was lost on the hill." She grinned disbelievingly but mended the fire while I found my best leather jacket and put it on, then as I turned to leave she began to whine, "Bring me a cake, master, bring me something when you come back from the feast. I should be in the kitchen, helping with the other women, but my man was killed in a raid two seasons ago and they sent me here because there was no one to speak for me. And who wants to sit alone in this hut when they have roasted an ox, and there will be drinking and, after it, fighting?" Perhaps it was the flickering light that made her mouth so cruel? I shuddered and hurried outside, lest she clutch my arm to detain me longer.

The chief man of the village had lent Osmund his hall. It was already so crowded that the only bench left empty was near the entrance. The captains and the Irish chiefs were sitting beside the fire in the center of the room, arranged according to precedence, the fighters on one side, the elders on the other, but there was no ceremony as far as the crews were concerned: we sat where we liked among our friends. It reminded me of the King's palace at Lestowder where I had often served at similar feasts as a boy. The priests wore white robes and one had a chain of twisted links around his neck but Osmund had followed the Irish custom: the higher the rank, the gayer the colors. The skin door slipped from my hand in my astonishment as I saw him. He had risen for some reason and the torches above, the firelight below, had turned his beard, his arm-bands and his coat into such magnificence that he seemed to be a figurehead of gold.

One serf brought me bread, another ladled a portion of meat on top of it and as I had eaten nothing since the early morning I forgot my woes for half an hour, making up for my long fast. Oh, how pleasant it would be to go to my rushes and sleep, I thought, still a little dismally, after I had stuffed the last morsel into my mouth. It was impossible to move, however, until we had toasted the New Year, the harvest and our ships. I saw a man stripping the cover from his harp and hoped that he would sing of some voyager rather than the ancient kings. Few of us could understand the language and we would rather have talked but perhaps, as I had heard Osmund say, it kept us from quarrelling after the ale.

A number of hounds were waiting behind us. I flung my last bone to one of them and as its jaw snapped over it the door at my elbow opened. A wind must have begun to blow because the cold blast flicked my legs and a man's cloak blew forward and knocked over a cup. Another guest tramped in heavily, his shoulders sprinkled with snow. He looked round and, to my surprise, took the vacant seat beside me; he was a full steersman with the right to sit much further up the room. "No," he growled, noticing my amazement, "after losing my way in these hills, I want meat first and compliments afterwards. You are a silent fellow and will leave me alone until I've eaten."

I nodded, I knew the man slightly and liked him although many were afraid of him. He came from the North, a full week's sail beyond the Frisians, and it was rumored that he could talk to the winds. Opinions differed as to whether it were wise to have him for a shipmate, strange things had been known to happen to people whom he disliked. I thought that I could understand his knowledge. The climate in his land was so harsh that even babies learned to notice some tiny change that was the forerunner of a storm. He was rough and hearty, exactly like the rest of his fellow sailors, only once, as he had begun to speak about the drift of tides, he had reminded me of a Gaul, an illusion dispelled the next moment when he had shouted, "And who will keep me warm tonight?" as boisterously as any of us to a passing fisherman's daughter.

"More ale?"

My companion shook his head. A slave happened to pass us with a torch and the light, falling on the transparent drinking horn, turned its contents (it was still half full) into gold. "I do not need drink to make me merry," he grinned and added, as if he too had noticed the similarity between the colors, "I want true metal and not a reflection of it, we can't hold the colors of the sky between our fingers."

"We all ask for wealth," I said, "yet what does it bring us but fear?" I looked up at the slave who was watching us. Poor fellow, he was the son of a farmer in Wales and if he had been a landless herdsman he would have taken to his heels and escaped. Melvas (for that was his name) had tried instead to save his father's oxen, so the raiders had seized him as well as the cattle.

"Where did you listen to such sermons, boy? Gold gives everything, freedom to the slave, a ship to me."

"I'm not a boy," I protested angrily, "I have five voyages behind me."

"You are, when you talk like a priest." He flung his head back with such a roar of laughter that with his great beard and tiny eyes, he resembled the dried head of the walrus that I had once seen on an Irish ship. Its owner had said that the beast must have been washed shorewards from the North.

"Gold makes feuds, any man will tell you that," and I quoted the proverb, "Too many rings sharpen a man's sword."

"Oh, it need not, it need not but you brawlers are stupid. If you only knew . . ." he broke the sentence off on purpose to arouse my curiosity.

"If I knew what?" It was on the tip of my tongue to ask him if he could really calm the winds but I remembered in time that he was supposed to punish those who questioned him about his gift. He stared at my face as if trying to decide whether I were trustworthy or not, then he said slowly, "We fight about gold because there is so little of it, yet whenever we brawl and a man is lost, there is one less to set the sails or till the fields. Oh, it is a sullen grandfather, this earth. It grows older and older. What would you say, boy, if we were to step backwards . . . or forwards . . . into the world's youth?"

He had been drinking, I thought, that was why he had come late but I was too lazy to quarrel, so I answered jokingly, "You were feasting at whose hall before you reached our table?"

The steersman smiled and shook his head. "I was up on the headland, watching the waves, and if my lips tasted anything, it was salt water. There was much spray but the wind won't last. It's as warm as our summer." The talk stopped suddenly while an elder stood up to pray, then as Osmund followed him with the first of the toasts we sprang up, shouted and drank. "Have you been often in Ireland?" my companion asked when we sat down again.

"This is my second winter."

"Then you must have heard about the voyagers at one of the feasts; the gods know that we have enough festivals here."

"I know the tale of Bran but though I can ask my way or bargain for eggs I cannot understand the ancient language that the singers use."

"In the winter you have plenty of time to learn, it is more useful than sleeping." He signed to Melvas, who came over with his jug, but there was such bitterness in the slave's face that I almost drew my drinking horn away for fear that he had poisoned the ale. My friend seemed not to notice; he undid a thong of his leather jacket and began to speak, not like a harper but in the way that a child will talk to itself, with little breaks and pauses, as if he were alone and did not expect me to listen to him.

"Bran was the most famous, yes, and there were hermits who sat on rocks and preached, I suppose, to seals but I know of seafarers who sailed to the islands at the rim of the world. They were men who had the sense to keep their mouths shut when they came back, so that those dreamers there," he nodded towards the singer who was standing at Osmund's elbow, "couldn't win bracelets with a tale about a floating kingdom or a stag with five legs. What does a man know about the sea until a wave has knocked him over and tried to roll him overboard?"

"Nothing," I agreed as positively as the Northerner could have wished. It was impossible to replace experience, imagination was not the same, the cold, the danger and the motion had to be felt by the body as well as the mind.

"Tell me about them," I begged. I was beginning to be interested in spite of my drowsiness.

"Not so fast, Ru-an, or is it Rune?" He made the usual joke. "Not every sailor can venture to the islands, they have to be chosen by the gods. By all of them, perhaps, because I've seen the Cross and the Mistletoe aboard the same vessel and my own amulet as well." He tapped the talisman that all Finns wore round their necks. "There is no quarrelling on the water as there is on land, it's a man's skill that counts in a storm and not his thoughts. Nor are these wanderers the people you would expect to find. Bran was a king, but he's the only one that I remember. I think, but mind you, this is merely my opinion, the gods give more to seekers than they do to raiders. Yes," he sighed, and ran his fingers through his thick hair, "I once knew a chief who had a hundred black cows and what did the fool do? He sold them to take an oar along with the rest, to look for a cream-colored calf with a star on its forehead." The Finn flung his head back in a second gale of laughter while I looked round uneasily but our neighbors were too busy drinking to notice us.

"If wandering is in you, you can no more stop it than you can the winds." I spilt some beer in horror as the words slid out, terrified that I had angered him.

113

"Sometimes you can tame them both," he answered but so gently that I knew he had forgiven me for my slip, "but not if you want to reach that island. A year there is no longer than a day." He looked at me to see if I would smile but I nodded and as I waited for him to continue the hall began to rock under me as if I were in a coracle and a fresh spring breeze were blowing away the smells of sweat, beer and smoke.

"There has to be the summons," the Finn continued. "Bran heard it through music or so the harpers say and we mustn't grudge them a jar or two of honey to sweeten their songs. We sailors know that it is the draw and fall of waves in a man's ears. Let him plow a field or sleep by the hearthstone, a time will come when his hands will itch for ropes." His voice dropped into the chant of just those storytellers whom he seemed to dislike but I did not laugh; the more restless the words, the more I felt at peace.

"And then?" I asked anxiously because he was leaning forward with his eyes fixed on the board in front of him as if he had nothing more to say.

"Not so fast, child of five notches."

"I never spoil a good oar," I answered disdainfully. Some men cut a mark whenever they made a voyage.

"First, the gods choose a leader. He listens and waits, it may be for years. He has to know his comrades and I don't mean his crew but the elements that will look after him."

I wondered if the Finn were prodding me to make an incautious reference to the winds but this time I remembered and was silent.

"Then he has to find a ship. It should have been built from timber blessed by the priests with a light helm and a deep hold. Those are the laws but actually," he looked at me solemnly but I saw that he was about to burst into a third yell of laughter, "one man I know went there in a skin-covered curagh, it was what you Cornish call a scath, and he wasn't looking for any island, he was blown there off his course. A ship, Ruan, needs gold."

I smiled and ventured to drink a little of my beer. How inconstant Man is! I had grumbled for weeks that I would sooner be under the earth than above it and now, simply because a fellow sailor was talking to me about islands, I was terrified that Melvas would poison me! The men round us seemed unconcerned. I looked at the slave and saw him smile at a jest in spite of himself and felt reassured. Alas, what strange tricks our imaginations play on us and how completely we are at their mercy!

"A captain without a crew is as lonely as our bard," the Finn pointed to the harper who was running his fingers restlessly along the rim of his small harp, "Watch, he is waiting until we are drunk enough to listen to him. The voyagers should be men with neither hawk nor home to call them back at the end of the year. They are bound to the islands if they find them. It is the usual sacrifice to the gods."

"You are a good storyteller," I said approvingly and I had had experience, "but if nobody returns, how do you know that it is a land of youth or . . . ," I looked at him, "gold?"

"Wait. You are trying to cast anchor before we have sailed. There are ordeals on the way and the last of them is not the most perilous. Men are scornful, and we have to slip away," he looked as if by chance at Osmund, whose face was now as red as the fire in front of him as he lifted a great, silver flagon to his lips. "Yes, that is the first danger and, to me, the worst."

I was sleepy again, as sleepy as we were after a great storm when we dropped exhausted beside the oars and even the bilge water rolling over our wet feet could not wake us up. I think I dreamed that I was back in the market place and that a voice was saying once more, *"Morcades, the mother of Gawain, sent a ship to fetch him to her island beyond the seas."* Suppose a story had been used to hide a fact? Then I think that the steersman must have nudged me because as I opened my eyes I heard him say, ". . . and ten days further we come to the place where all winds turn and we cannot understand each other."

I was careful not to reply and the Finn smiled. "You are a good listener, Ruan. You do not spring at a man for swearing a different oath to your own. Drink with me, there is no need to be afraid!"

"Hail!" The guests were on their feet, shouting and lifting their flagons to each other, but it was too noisy to hear the toast. We drank, stamped, and sat down again; it was a splendid feast. Osmund was a good leader and a generous man; the evening must be costing him half of his summer's earnings. "Suppose we escape our neighbors and the storms," I said, for I was following the Finn's story now with passionate interest, "is there another test?"

"There is the ice. It comes floating on a clear sea but, if it thickens and catches your vessel in its teeth, put your hands at your sides and go down with the ship. I once saw two bodies on a floe. They had jumped clear as it struck but the cold had taken their wits. There they lay, so alike that they must have been brothers, but each man's knife was in the other's chest and their faces were twisted with hatred. We thought that they were alive as we approached them but from the fashion of their garments they must have been dead for fifty years."

"I saw such floes on my second voyage but there were birds on them."

"Then your boat was near land."

"Yes, but we prayed all the same." We had been blown westward in the tail end of a gale, the year after I had left the Scillys. I had watched the dirty, white cakes floating towards us from every side and feared that I had brought disaster on the ship because I had defied my uncle's wishes. A breeze had come to drive us to the south and two days later, with the sun shining above the sparkling water, I had forgotten my terror. "Are there other dangers?" I asked.

"Ice and fog are the last ordeals on the sea, if the gods so will. What happens when you reach the island is another story and I may not speak of it."

I yawned; so it was just another seafaring tale to while away a winter hour and I felt cheated. "I know," I mocked, "you wake up and find yourself at home again." I did not wish him to think me credulous.

The Finn turned as if he were going to strike me, then

he must have seen my disappointment because he laughed. "You are right to doubt a man till you have tested his faith, Ruan, but I am not telling you lies. Call me Friedowald, because you will never pronounce my own name properly, and men have been calling me Friedowald for so long that it seems now to belong to me. Your captain is going to give a bracelet to that fellow for shouting at us about a battle that nobody remembers. Once my memory goes to sleep, you have to rattle silver in front of it to wake it up."

I searched inside the bag that hung from my belt but all I could find was a battered penny. I offered this to Friedowald but he shook his head. "I'll answer one question as a New Year gift but be quick with it, I'm tired."

"How many days' sailing is the island from here?"

"So you are a seaman?" Friedowald laughed. "Not, 'Are there women or where is the fountain of youth?' but a good practical inquiry. I see your curiosity has wakened you up." He threw the scraps and what remained of his bread to the waiting hounds, drank some beer slowly while I waited impatiently and then, with many grimaces because his fingers could not find it at first, he dragged a bone oblong from under his shirt. It was covered with points and lines that seemed merely ornamental and it hung from a whale-hide loop. "Well, can you decipher it?" he inquired.

"Those are not runes." I could not read them but I knew the shape of the strokes.

He tapped the right corner. A badly drawn stag was

grazing in a circle no bigger than a nail. Then he drew his short, brown finger across to the opposite side and I managed to make out a walrus head, though it was indicated rather than carved, with black points pricked irregularly below its tusks. "My map," he explained and I stared at him almost in horror. We knew that there were men who had such charts in their possession but they guarded them as a king his only daughter or his treasure. "And you show this to a stranger?" I exclaimed.

"You cannot read it."

"That is true but I might steal it from you."

"Nobody knows its secret but myself. Besides, Ruan, I have never shown it except to three men, and they, I hope, will sail with me."

"And I will be the fourth," I shouted joyfully. Was it possible that this strange voyage was linked up with the questions that had baffled me so much while I was dreaming in my hiding place? The present was as dense as one of Friedowald's fogs but for some unfathomable reason I was happy.

"Can you pay your share? I can have a queen with her maids and six embroidered robes for the price of one ship and, for myself, I prefer the vessel. I might take you, say, for three silver bracelets."

"I risked death every day for five months to get as many links and we called it a good voyage."

"Bring whatever you have to me next spring but I warn you I shall choose the richer fellows first." His eyes twinkled in his wrinkled face until he looked more like an old mastiff than a sailor. He opened his shirt and slipped the chart inside it at the very moment when the board was pushed back so suddenly that we almost fell off our benches. "Darts! Those shepherd playthings! Men use axes." One of the Frisians was banging his fist on the table, they could never hold their ale. He brushed his companion's arm aside and roared out sneeringly, "They jump on your back here from behind a tree. They daren't meet us weapon to weapon."

"Will you fight?" Nera, a chief's son, sprang to his feet. He had just been accepted as a member of Moram's bodyguard and had come home to feast his success.

"Take the child's knife away, he may cut himself," the Frisian jeered.

"Quiet," Osmund thundered from the center table, "the harper is waiting to sing to us."

"They can run like hares but they can't swing an ax," the fellow repeated drunkenly. He held out his thorn to be refilled but Ligulf, a sworn brother though no kinsman, shoved the slave away.

"Quiet!" Osmund shouted again, rapping the table with the palm of his hand. "The man's drunk, it's a form of homesickness," he added loudly to the Irish beside him; none of us wanted the incident to develop into a brawl.

Ligulf dragged his friend back onto the bench while the men around them tried to laugh the matter off. Nera was still on his feet, in the gay, mixed colors permitted to the bodyguard, but his brother had him by the wrist and was trying to calm his rage. All would have been well if I had not heard a familiar voice proclaim to a neighboring table, "This place has become a nest of Frisians. Still, it's natural for a girl to prefer a man who has given three cows for her to a hunter full of lice."

Nera's face turned a violent red, he sprang forward and hit the Frisian, who he had mistakenly supposed was jeering at him again, full in the mouth. A board fell, the beer flowed over the floor and our apparent friendliness vanished in a moment.

"I did not know that Lydd was here," I muttered angrily to Friedowald. I had looked round for him but had not seen him. "It was a deliberate provocation because while Nera was absent for his training, a sailor gave a big bride price for the girl he had expected to marry."

People yelled in half a dozen languages, we gathered or were pressed into two groups, one at each end of the hall, an overturned torch set fire to some of the rushes. It was usual to settle quarrels the day after they had happened because when the men had recovered from their drunkenness it was often possible to arrange a dispute with jests and a mutual exchange of gifts but there was so much anger in the air that sooner than risk a general battle both Moram and Osmund shouted that the men were to fight immediately outside the hall. Friedowald and I were too far away to hear more than cries and orders but we were swept outside with the rest towards a flat, open space a little to the left of the building. Boys rushed to get fresh torches, and a moment later, although there was no moon, the square seemed almost as bright as day. I looked at the darkness behind me and shivered.

The grotesque faces, the blazing leaves, the crunch of a fallen drinking horn under a man's foot, reminded me of being woken by a squall one night and seeing a wave of black water about to crash on our ship.

"It's murder," I muttered, "they are both so drunk that they can hardly stand on their legs."

"It *is* to be darts," a steersman shouted.

"Darts first and then axes."

There was a loud, angry shout, "I'll fight the fool with any weapons he likes," followed by Ligulf's protest, "The ax, man, have you lost your senses, choose the ax."

Friedowald turned to me in bewilderment. "What does he mean?" he asked.

"Nera has just passed his test for the bodyguard," I explained. "He had to stand in an open space while nine of Moram's men flung darts at him from between the trees. Each had to be caught on his shield and if he got a single scratch on his arm he failed. The Irish practice hurling as soon as they can walk and the dart is a deadly weapon in their hands. The only chance for the Frisian is to stick to the weapon he knows."

"Two pennies," people were shouting, "two pennies to this belt on the Frisian." It was a relic, I suppose, of my uncle's training but I had no stomach to wager pence on a man's life. Some of our best fighters disliked these drunken contests. It usually meant that a ship had to sail short-handed in the spring.

"This on the Frisian," one of the crew said, holding up a silver buckle, but I shook my head. "I've already wagered what I have," I lied, as I pushed my way forward with Friedowald following me until we stood in the front line on the far side of the square. The Irish stood opposite us but the two ends, behind each combatant, were left free on account of the darts. "The Frisian!" his fellow sailors shouted, stamping their feet. "The Frisian!" He swaggered up to a position close to where I was standing and grinned. His face was flushed, a lock of almost yellow hair straggled from under the rim of his leather, metal-studded cap. He belonged to the other ship that was wintering in the harbor. I had often seen him and doubted that he was more than nineteen. The Irish yelled something in their own tongue that I could not understand. "What are they saying?" Friedowald asked and I shrugged my shoulders. "I do not like it, he may have been in the wrong but they are so drunk it will be no test of skill but pure luck."

"It is always luck," Friedowald looked at me curiously, "you cannot change customs, however stupid, unless . . ."

"You find a new island." We smiled, like conspirators, at each other.

Osmund stepped forward to declaim the conditions of the fight and after he had finished the chief repeated it in Irish. The hot, excited murmurs about us gradually stilled. "What is it to be?" I whispered to the man the other side of me, "I could not hear."

"Something for both sides. First three darts, but afterwards axes."

Osmund held up his staff. There was dead silence. The Frisian's friends stepped back and he stood there in a metal-studded coat with a painted shield in front of his body. He looked gigantic in the torchlight and, by contrast, the Irish boy seemed smaller in his borrowed leather than he was in reality. "Who do you think will win?" Friedowald asked, "I'm not asking for a wager, just for your opinion."

"Nera spent the summer in the hills, living on berries or what he could shoot with a small bow and arrow. Nobody dared give him even a crust of bread. He had to race through the undergrowth and take a thorn from his foot while he ran, with all his comrades after him. If he had slackened speed and they had caught him, they had the right to do anything short of killing him. He is drunk now, it is true, but his hand is still skillful." Friedowald smiled and I wondered if he had put the question to me as a test? "You use your eyes," he answered, pushing forward a little, "and are not content with echoing your comrades' words." Just then, the crews around us began to shout that it was murder rather than a match, how could that scraggy boy stand up against the Frisian giant?

Osmund lifted his staff a second time and again said something that I could not hear.

He waited a moment, thrust the staff upward in a third, final gesture and almost before his hand had fallen to his side there was the whistle of a dart through the air. The Frisian caught it on the extreme rim of his shield but so narrowly that it splintered and fell in several pieces at his feet. He threw his own weapon angrily and clumsily. Nera did not try to catch it, he simply stooped and it passed harmlessly over his head. There was a prolonged roar from the crowd.

I looked round uneasily, wondering what would happen if the battle rage gained our lines? We might be better armed but a falling brand could easily set the village on fire and then the Irish could disappear into their woods and wait until we were too weak with hunger to defend ourselves. I could see that Osmund was anxious, he shifted his fingers restlessly up and down his staff, or flung his cloak impatiently away from his arm. "Lift the torches higher," he ordered unnecessarily although they were beginning to burn down, and I saw that the captain of the Frisian's ship looked puzzled and angry.

The shadowy figures of the combatants moved into a square of light from the darkness to which one of them was shortly to return. The Northman swung into position and caught the point of Nera's javelin this time magnificently in the center of his shield. We yelled with joy, and in a moment of vanity he lowered his buckler and grinned. At that immediate second Nera hurled the third dart. It caught the Frisian full in the throat; we heard the clang of metal on the ground before we realized that he had fallen. "Alas," Friedowald whispered, "you were right. Men should stick to the weapons they know."

There was a howl of dismay, not only from the Frisian's comrades but from other sailors who had lost their wagers. "The feast is over," Osmund yelled, "go to your huts." I heard the harper's voice rise above the din, ordering his countrymen to disperse. There was a moment's hesitation but we were sobered by the deadly speed of the Irish javelins, and though there was some muttering, groups formed quickly to prevent the reckless fools among us from seizing their arms.

Ligulf was kneeling by his friend. There was nothing that he, or any of us, could do. I looked away from the face and the great limbs that were as twisted now as any water rat's body transfixed by some chance arrow. He had been an orphan, at least there was nobody but his shipmates to mourn for him; they stood round him in a circle, each praying according to his fashion, while the boys extinguished the torches and somebody flung an old sack over the body. "Go to your huts," Osmund roared again. The old year had ended, the new had begun its irrevocable pattern. Friedowald touched my arm, we turned and followed the groups that were walking down the frosty path. A pebble rolled against another stone, a dog barked, there was the occasional slap of a hide as a man pushed past it towards his sleeping place. Nobody spoke. I think that we were glad of the darkness. It hid the fears that we did not want to acknowledge to each other, the voyages to come, the briefness of the feast, and all the wild, unknown immensity of night and fate.

One day it was spring; the next it was almost winter again but the year had turned, the days were longer, and though we grumbled we were happier after Osmund had ordered us to the shore, to prepare the *Seagull* for another voyage. We had left her well covered but there was always a corner where the rain had seeped through some join, there might be a plank to change on one of the

126

rowing benches or a leaking water cask. If the weather were fine, or there were a light, drying wind we spread the sails on the grass beside the beach, then our sail-maker, on his hands and knees, went over them inch by inch.

Friedowald had gone to a port about twenty miles up the coast. To tell the truth, I had almost forgotten him. It was easy to dream about islands on a bleak December night, but now, as we scraped and polished, I was part of the crew again, caught up in a pattern, in a world to ourselves where Osmund was king, far from landsmen quarrelling over stolen cattle or a boundary stone. It was hard work; we had to drag the tubs up to the shingle to a spot where we could dry and scour them, our tools often broke and it rained the whole day when we were mending the scow but the worst disaster that I could imagine was to lose my place in the ship. Alfgar could whine his stories again that had irritated me during the winter, I could laugh at them now with the rest.

"Why did I go to sea?" The man beside me scratched some weed from the hull with an old flint scraper be-cause the salt spoiled our knives and looked mournfully at the long space to be cleaned. "As soon as I begin to catch up on my sleep, out we tumble into the cold again, scrubbing and rubbing, rubbing and scrubbing, just to be able to risk our necks, beating up the Channel."

"It is better than having to get up on an icy morning to pasture the cows."

"One day we shall take a Faroe ship," a boy said confidently, he was the son of an Irish father and a

127

Welsh mother and about to make his first voyage, "then we should come back with gold and could buy ourselves farms."

"Not with Osmund," Alfgar said, looking round hastily to see who had overheard him.

"They say he has made a bargain again with the Irish merchants and we shall cross to Brittany with the fleet."

"We may earn less but it's a safer journey," the steersman said, tapping a plank with the handle of his knife. "It suits me better than coming to blows with a raider; since I got an arrow through my arm, I can't lift a shield."

"One day we shall all be food for whales and even our mothers will not recognize us."

"One day," somebody shouted from the edge of the circle, "I shall find a girl who will make me forget the oar blisters on my palm for a whole night."

The talk went on, spreading from one to the other, yet if Moram had offered us land, none of us would have accepted an acre. We were a unity, moving together as if we were a single pair of oars. Unlike the steersman, I often wondered if this were not the happiest time of the year? The launching of a ship had the quality of a boy's dream without the harshness of the first week at sea when our hands were soft and our bellies whimpered for fresh and shore-cooked food.

It must have been midafternoon when a messenger came up and asked for our captain. We knew the man, he came from the next port, and while someone went to fetch Osmund we offered him some dried meat. "What is your news?" Alfgar asked, he was always curious, as we stood round the newcomer in a circle.

"We had the fever badly this year," the man answered between mouthfuls, "they say it was the rains."

"It has been a dreadful winter," Ligulf answered. He had never recovered from the shock of his friend's death.

"Five died, and we should have lost more, but we had an Irish leech wintering with us and he had a new remedy."

"Not a yellow draught, almost the color of beer?"

"Yes, though it did not taste like it. It increased the fever for a while but a day or two later the patient woke up without an ache in his bones."

"It is full of Irish magic," Ligulf exclaimed, "I would rather die than taste it, it binds the drinker to this soil." Since the fight, he had talked incessantly of his home.

"No, it was simply feverfew," I answered, "we have been using it in Cornwall for as long as I can remember."

"Watch and wait. The men who took it will never leave this country," Ligulf thumped the cask that he was mending with his fist. "Besides, when a man is sick, he has done something to offend the gods. It is better to make a sacrifice."

I did not reply but began to untwist some rope. Honorius had warned us to be patient when a peasant had preferred to rub his sores against the bark of a holy tree instead of taking the salves that Kaden had offered him. "It is easier for him to think that his poisoned hand has come from neglect of an offering than because he grasped a thorn bush in the dark, chasing one of his master's hares." A gull cawed and I remembered running down the quay after Dungarth, not knowing then that I had seen my uncle for the last time.

"How many ships are they fitting out?" We all looked up in surprise. Only Alfgar with his mixture of cunning and stupidity could have asked such an ill-mannered question. Of course we wanted to know which captain would be the first to leave because he would get the pick of the cargoes but it was a dangerous remark and few sailors would have answered it.

"Three. There is my master's boat, we should be ready in another two weeks. Then there is the Scottish vessel that was dismasted last autumn but it will be another month before she is seaworthy."

"And the third?"

"Oh, the *Walrus*. Her owner was one of the people who died from the fever but he was too old ever to have taken her out again. The widow is coming with us, she is British and wants to return to her kinsfolk. She sold the hulk to a Finn for half its value."

"Was the man's name Friedowald?" I inquired.

"That or something like it. Perhaps you can tell me where he is going?"

"I! No! But he sat beside me at the New Year feast."

"The man is mad," Alfgar said, leaning on a paddle instead of oiling it. "I heard him talking about an island on the rim of the world."

"I should have smashed my fist in his face if I had heard such foolishness," Ligulf said angrily, "something happened at that feast to anger the gods."

"Why should it matter if some of us go exploring?" I asked, more out of curiosity than because I wanted to argue. I was glad that Friedowald had found a boat but I did not envy him his journey.

"Because a man inherits his father's tasks. He can sail or he can plow. Besides, if there had been another island worth the taking, our rulers would have sent a fleet there already. But you are Cornish and therefore half brother to the Irish," Ligulf added contemptuously, "their magic does not harm you."

"Sometimes a man has to be the one to chart the way as our ancestors found when they came here first in their coracles. Why do the gods send dreams to us unless they mean us to follow them?"

"Dreams? What has a sailor to do with dreams?" Alfgar rubbed a cloth dipped in fish oil slowly up and down the paddle. "Ligulf is right. A man should follow his father's occupation."

"Peace," our steersman said firmly, he was a quiet man who hated quarrels, "can't you see that Friedowald has spread such stories so that he can slip away and get a cargo while you are gossiping instead of checking the oars?"

"It's true!" The messenger laughed and wiped his mouth on his sleeve. "His old *Walrus* looks exactly like a duck. We can give him three days' start and overtake him in mid-ocean." Everybody laughed.

"Does the woman in the third house beyond the waterfront still sell her stagnant water under the name of mead?" Our sailmaker strolled up to the edge of the

group and dumped a piece of damaged leather on the
ground. I stepped aside as they began to joke again and
tried to untwist a length of rope that would be needed
for our anchor. "Something is wrong," I said to the
steersman who walked over to help me. "My grandfather
would have sailed on any adventure but all men want to
do now is to repeat their voyages, over and over."

"It's only natural, Ruan," the spiral of rope jerked
away from my comrade's hands and he licked his fingers,
"whenever a man breaks a pattern, he is changing his
companions' lives as well as his own. Would you like it
yourself? Who will your captain be this summer? Osmund or Friedowald?"

"Osmund, of course." Ligulf ran over to grab the
middle of the rope and held it taut while the steersman
wound his end onto a new block of wood. Whatever he
might think of me, we were as one while we were working on the ship. "You see," the steersman said, walking
towards me as he coiled, "the thong was wound so tightly
all the winter that it tugged against being straightened.
The familiar is stronger than the unknown."

I nodded as I looked from face to face. I had had
friends and there would be others outside the crew but
the sea bound us together in a way that no landsman
could understand. We were familiar with dangers that
did not frighten us any more while an unruly horse or
a night in the woods now seemed more terrifying than
in childhood. The grass was full of pebbles that had
stuck to our wet shoes, a white, broken shell lay on a
patch of earth. "I told her I would not give a pilchard for

the stuff," the messenger said gaily but before I had time to ask what some old woman had offered him I saw Osmund stride up to the circle and heard him shout angrily above the din, "Get on with mending those water casks and leave your gossiping till nightfall. Do you want us to be the last ship out of this harbor?"

Moram's house was a place of contrasts. The armor hanging on the wall was finer than anything that I had seen in Cornwall and the bowl standing at his elbow was worth two of our farms, yet nobody had troubled to clean out the yard and the stench of stale water and animal droppings was such that I wondered how the people round me could eat and sleep in such polluted air. The autumn hunting had been poor along the coast but as there had been plenty of game in the inland forest that covered half the kingdom, Osmund had sent me over to buy some meat before we sailed. The storekeeper had shown me a double line of hams hanging from the rafters in a neighboring barn but I realized that I had come too late, the King had already been drinking for several hours.

Moram leaned forward in the glow of the fire. He was a huge man, as tall as Osmund but much heavier; they said that he had been a better runner than Nera in his youth but now his calves bulged out of the hunting boots and his belly was wider than his ample coat. "Tell your captain," he snapped the words at me, "we are short of food but we are also hospitable. I will let him have five hams for five silver links."

It was the price of a good field and I let my astonishment flow into my voice. "Five links! But we are poor sailors, if we had so much silver we should not risk our lives along your coast."

"Poor!" Moram lifted his head and I saw why even Lydd was afraid of him. He had only to lift a finger and either of the guards standing beside his chair would seize me, thrash me, or fling me into the darkness among the barking dogs to find a perilous way home. "Poor! Well, if your master is as short of silver as you say, I will give him a ham in charity for the cloak he wore at the New Year feast, it is a pity to soak so gay a garment in salt water."

It was an insult but I had to keep my temper. "My master does not tell his men what he has in his chest. I will give him your message." I bowed and would have gone, dangerous though it was to leave the village at nightfall, but he remembered, I suppose, that a messenger had a right to the laws of hospitality and he turned to a boy standing behind his chair and told him contemptuously to find me a corner where I could sleep. Then he lifted his drinking horn as if by this gesture he had handed me some princely gift and I slipped away while his attention was fixed upon his beer.

The boy led me over to the furthest part of the hall and left me without a word. The rushes were filthy, there were scraps of gristle that even the dogs would not eat, husks and the skeleton of a small fish scattered among the stalks. I would sooner have slept on the hard but cleaner floor but I had to follow my neighbors' habits

134

unless I wanted a quarrel. A couple of youths asked me if I had come to join them because I was afraid of the sea but I smiled and pretended to be unable to under-stand them. I was about to roll myself up in my cloak when a familiar voice whispered from the corner, "Wait a moment, I will share my dinner with you," and Lydd sat down beside me on top of the fish bones and a mess of dirty crumbs.

"You should have come to me," he said reproachfully, handing me a slab of bread. "The King hates strangers but I might have got you some hams directly from the storekeeper; now it is too late."

"I looked for you, Lydd, but nobody knew where you were." I did not add that I had made no effort to find him.

"It's true. He sent me out to one of the farms to fetch a lamb," Lydd jerked his head towards Moram's chair, "then he forgot he had sent me and clouted me for lazi-ness when I got back. He's in a rage about something today."

"So I noticed. He asked a link of silver for a single ham."

Lydd laughed and offered me his drinking horn. "We will take turn and turn about," he said, "because there will be no filling it up this evening. I think his daughter's marriage is on his mind."

"They said that she was going to marry a chief's son from up the coast."

"Was, yes. The youth came and there are old women here who say the couple liked each other too swiftly and too well but Moram asked so heavy a bride price that, like yourself with the hams, the boy left. The King was disappointed but he already grudged the dozen cows that the bridal feast would have cost him and muttered he would have to find a richer man. He won't unless he hurries. The girl is getting old."

"We have taken nothing from his land," I said thoughtfully, "and Osmund's offer was one that any captain might make yet I thought he was going to order his guards to thrash me."

"Osmund's chest was full of silver when you landed and it suited Moram to have you guarding the harbor. He will be friendly enough next autumn when he hopes that you will winter here again and spend your wages. Meantime, it's spring. The earth is rich but we are poor." Lydd scooped up the last scrap of a bowl of stew that he had not offered to share with me and laughed.

"Yet you like his service."

"Like!" Lydd looked up scornfully. "Like! No free-born man likes to be thrashed for a slight fault nor to have his food flung to him as if he were a dog. I am more faithful to him than those famous guards of his—Nera, one day, will plunge a dart through his neck—but that is because your uncle trained me to be neither farmer, trader nor smith and I had no more stomach than you to be a priest."

It was the smoke but I thought for a moment that Lydd was asking me to pity him and how, I wondered, could Honorius ever have understood this wild creature whose ways were so different from his own? "A man always wants to impose his own will of life upon his pupils," I suggested quietly. "Can you imagine my uncle ever going willingly to a hunt?"

"Why do you always defend him?" I thought Lydd was going to spring, wolflike, at my throat. "I saved your skin and, without knowing it, your uncle's as well. What would have happened if you had both gone back to Lestowder?"

I nodded; in the world's view I ought to have been obedient and if Erbin had ever heard of my flight it would have grieved him, in spite of the fact that eventually it had turned out to be better for us all. I had spent watch after watch, all the same, struggling with a sense of guilt and the yoke that Honorius had imposed upon me was still the root of much of my restlessness. I could not join my companions in their simple pleasures nor dream their dreams. "What a trick you played on me," I said, trying to turn the conversation to a less dangerous subject, "I shall never forget waking up among a lot of strangers and finding you were not on board."

The grin on Lydd's curious, shrunken mouth turned almost into a scowl. "I never had a head for rough seas, I am too much the runner not to ask for earth under my toes."

"Do you never want to go back to Cornwall?"

"Why? When your uncle was at the height of his power, he could have bound me to a trader for a coin or two. I should have liked life, riding up and down the country from fair to fair. But now, unless Moram is in one of his rages, I have fire and food, a badge the farmers respect and friends. Why should I move?"

"I sometimes wish I could end my days at Godrevy," I really meant the islands and to have Erbin at my side again though I did not like to speak of this, "but the King and my brother would turn me out."

"I am an outcast and you have an elder brother," Lydd laughed, "we are twins."

There was a shout. King Moram had fallen forward over the board. His two guards were trying to lift him up and help him to his sleeping place while he yelled curses at them and shouted for the whip. "He won't last long," Lydd muttered with the same triumphant look that I had seen when he had provoked the Irish boy at our feast. "Nera likes me," he added, as if he had guessed my thoughts. Then he wriggled with a long, continuous movement out of the straw. "I have to sleep at the King's feet," he continued, "in case he wants a messenger. You should have come to me first, there is nothing now that I can do about the meat but you will forget your hunger as soon as you are in port. We shall meet in the autumn, I expect, and meantime, a happy voyage." He stepped over the two men snoring beside us, waved to me and disappeared among the men further up the hall. What a pity my uncle had so misunderstood us, I thought, as I rolled my cloak round me; under all his cunning, Lydd seemed to have a loyal and generous heart.

April was almost over. The thorn was out, the turf was as full of flowers as grass, all the roots in the moist and sun-warmed earth were growing again. I had neither a rope nor scraper in my hand and strolled along, knowing that this was the last holiday that I should have till the end of summer, watching the birds and the tight, rolled-up fists of the furze blossoms, without a thought of danger.

"Have you a scrap of leather on you?" a voice asked. I looked up to see an old man sitting on a bank, fumbling with a broken strap on his shoe. His shepherd's crook was lying at his side. The peasants believed that the sailors were richer than themselves and were always begging us for bits of wood and hide. I searched in my wallet but could only find a bit of twine. "Will this do?" I asked. "It is all I have."

The shepherd took it gratefully and measured it in his hands. "Are you going back to the coast? If so, take the path to the left and it will save you an hour's climb."

It was rare for the village people to tell us of their short cuts. They feared, with some reason, that we might spoil their hunting or even pick up a lamb. I thanked him and strolled on, the way that he had suggested skirted a forest. I noticed a sanctuary on the top of a low hill and its circle of trees brought back a drowsy morning at Lestowder. Honorius had taken us for once instead of Kaden and had begun to talk to us about our future duties. "Your robe will protect you," he had said, "but every valley has its customs. Always take a guide with you if you can but if you are alone avoid the woods. There may be a thicket among them where even a King's messenger is unwelcome."

139

It was good advice but the day was hot, I was thirsty and when I heard the rustle of a stream I left the track and thrust my way across the undergrowth until I found it, splashing into an oblong hollow rather than a pool, with banded, jewellike pebbles glistening under the shallow water. I put my hand on a great fern that was slowly forcing two stones apart and stooped but before I could swallow a mouthful a girl's voice said mockingly, "What a hunter! Drinking at noon! No wonder we are short of meat." It was the custom in Ireland for men and particularly for Moram's guards to drink only at sunrise or after sunset.

"I do not think you will starve," I grunted, with my memory full of that barn stuffed with hams. I glanced round but the place appeared to be empty, there were no footprints on the wet rocks nor any sign that the bushes had been disturbed. I shrugged my shoulders and was about to continue my journey when something, I thought for an instant that it was a wild cat, sprang from the bough of a tree to block my path. "A child could hide from you," the voice continued mockingly, "what do sailors do at sea? Sleep?"

It was a girl of perhaps sixteen and she had been able to hide from me because of her dress. It was the exact color of the growing leaves mixed with enough rust and brown to tone in with the branches. Her face was sunburnt but smooth, it had not the leathery quality of skin that we noticed on the herders' children who were sent to follow the flocks almost as soon as they could walk nor did she speak like a peasant. "What are you

140

doing here?" I answered rudely because I was annoyed that she had seen me search the thicket for her. "You were not sent into this wood to mind cows."

"How do you know?" she laughed, "Are you a Fili, can you tell me my future?"

"I do not need to be a Fili," I was secretly flattered at being asked if I were a seer, "I can guess this by your skin and your voice."

"What a pity! It is lonely here and I hoped that you might know what this new summer is to bring me?" She pulled a cloak down from the tree behind her, folded it and sat down on the edge of the pool with her bare legs dangling in the water.

"Why don't you return to the village?" I asked suspiciously, it was unusual for a solitary girl to wander so far from the huts.

"I can't." She looked round at me a little sulkily. "My mistress has gone up to the sanctuary with the priest and her uncle. They will be there for another hour."

I knew then that she was an attendant upon King Moram's daughter but I was still surprised that they had left her alone. "I wonder that you have no companion with you," I continued, "are you not afraid to be here by yourself?"

"In the sacred wood? Nobody would dare to touch me here." She drew back with a bewildered look and added anxiously, "But you, you are a stranger."

"You have nothing to fear," I assured her, "I am Cornish and know the rites."

"Cornish! Then what are you doing with that noisy

band of barbarians? I know now who you are. Your captain sent you over to us yesterday but is such a miser that he grudged us the low price we asked for our meat."

"You seem to know more about me than I do myself," I answered with some amusement.

"Oh, the storekeeper told us when we went to fetch the water." She brushed a lock of hair away from her forehead; it was as black as the apple seeds we used to crunch as children. "If you come from Cornwall what are you doing on that Northerner's ship? Tell me about the past as I see you know nothing of the future."

"It's a long story and I must be on my way." We were several miles from either Moram's village or the coast and if some malicious shepherd saw me alone with a girl there might be trouble. It was a favorite trick to fine a sailor just as his ship was about to leave and, although Osmund would pay it for me or for any other of his crew, I did not want to work all summer for nothing.

"If you belonged to our people, you would not be so rude. We are inside the enclosure, not on the highway." The girl looked at me so reproachfully that I hesitated. "There," she pointed to a large, flat boulder, "wait and talk to me for a few minutes. My sister was to have come with me but she woke up this morning with a fever and I am too old now to sit like a baby, plaiting garlands."

It was hot, a rest was welcome and I sat down; a moment would not matter, I pretended to myself, I was doing no harm and, looking at the girl who was pulling something that she had hidden from behind a clump of bracken, I decided that her apparent boldness was simply innocence. The flowering grasses flung a bell-shaped shadow on the opposite stones, there were tiny silver hairs inside the leaves of a water plant near my elbow and I forgot my uneasiness completely when she handed me a hunk of dried deer's tongue on a large slab of bread. They had given me no breakfast in the village and I had been too proud to ask for the food that by the laws of hospitality they should have offered me. "Isn't this worth a story?" she teased, tossing some crumbs to a bird.

I felt strangely shy. How could I speak about the dirt and perils of our voyages to so young a girl? I told her instead of a pig that we had had at Godrevy, whose tail had curled into the exact shape of a saucer and about the infant who had sold me the necklace of shells. "Enjoy your summer," I continued as solemnly as any old man, "the seasons return but childhood vanishes. It is like the bonewort that turns a field into a blue and white cloth one summer and is gone the next. You will not be able to loiter in the woods when you have a husband."

To my surprise, the girl laughed and pulled an edge of skirt over her knees as if she had just realized that they were uncovered. "I did not give you a piece of the King's own venison to be told about a childhood that I have already outgrown and, to be truthful, never valued. Why did you leave Cornwall to sail in a Northern ship? Had you been outlawed?"

It would have been simpler to say yes but I shook my head. I was about to speak of Agnas but some remnant of my training and respect for my oath made me turn instead to my first voyage. "It was late in the year and I had to winter in Wales. They burn a dried heather there that makes a lot of smoke, it is different from the peat that you use here." Then the years floated round in my head until I was drunk with memories and the sound of my own voice, perhaps I borrowed an incident or two that had really happened to a shipmate, but if so, I was simply following a harper's example and taking my material where I needed it. I left out the northeast wind that brought sores to our faces and described instead how we had run before the wind across short blue waves full of floating, golden jellyfish to join the Brittany fleet and as, in listening, she drew nearer to me it was natural to find that my arm was round her waist. "I understand now why you did not want to wait with me," she murmured, "I did not know that you were the son of a chief."

"I am only a steersman now," I answered, omitting the word "second." She was unlikely to meet any of my comrades.

"I wish I could see Cornwall," she sighed.

"You must marry a sailor and he will take you there. We had an Irish girl in our village."

"I cannot leave my mistress until after her wedding and her father waits until he can find a man twice her age who can offer him two hundred cows. Now if she were to marry somebody like yourself . . ."

"I cannot marry anybody, I have no silver."

"Perhaps you have never met the right girl," she mocked as she threaded a white flower into the thong of my coat; "not all of us want rings."

"But your fathers want cattle." I flung a pebble into the water and as I watched the ripples disappear I asked, to change so dangerous a subject, "And your mistress, is she kind to you? How does she treat you?"

"She prays too much but she leaves me alone. It's her foster mother whom the women dread. She has a tongue that is worse than a whip and she never stops scolding us. If I were a sailor like you, I should leave with the fleet and never come back."

I could smell the scent in her hair from the shrubs where she had been lying, was it bracken, was it gorse? "There are other things in life than pulling oars," I said and I swear that I meant no more than to tease her with a kiss or two, as I had played with the girls on my brother's farm. She jerked her face away, her headcloth fell towards the water and as we tried to save it we both began to slide down the bank. I grasped her to keep her from rolling, she laughed, the cloth drifted away and a moment later we found ourselves lying happily together in each other's arms.

A sound rapped across my drowsy ears. "Wake up!" the girl shook me anxiously, "My mistress is coming. The priest is lame and I can hear his stick." I listened as I sprang up and snatched my cloak; they could not be far away. "Promise to meet me here in two days," she begged while I flicked a crumb or two from her hair. "They will go back then to finish the ceremony."

"At the same hour?" She nodded and I swore by all

145

the sailor oaths I knew that she would not have to wait for me.

"Hurry!" She pushed me towards the thicket but as I stooped to give her a last kiss something moved (could it have been a cap?) between the two thin saplings on the other side of the pool. There was no time to search the place and I raced into the undergrowth, lost my way, found a clump of bracken that I remembered having left to my right, skirted its edge and came out on the small path. What a fool I had been to take the girl for a child! I had not been her first lover nor would I be her last but it had been a lucky meeting and some consolation for my failure to get the meat; Osmund was strict with us and kept us away from the villages. "If you want to marry," he would roar, "wait till the voyage is over and you are back with your own people."

I had both the earth and the sea around me when I came within sight of our harbor, an hour after I had left the wood. A scent of crushed bracken filled the air where some startled cattle had trodden it down that morning and the waves followed each other with the rapid beat of oars along the sand. The track happened to pass within a short distance of my winter hiding place and as it was still early I thought that I would rest there for a moment. If Osmund flew into one of his rages because of my news, I wanted to dig up my savings that had been buried for safety in the burrow, in case he did not let me leave my shipmates again. The gods must have sent this thought to me, otherwise I should have walked straight to my doom.

146

There was no sign of disturbance when I got to the hole except that some of the grass had blown away during the spring gales. It took me longer than I had expected to pry the bowl out from under some roots and empty it on the ground. I sat down to count the contents; I still had the five gold links that my uncle had given me because some scruple had kept me from using them even during my first, hard days in Wales. I had, besides, a dozen pieces of silver; it was a meager enough reward for all the *Seagull's* dangers. I slipped a couple of bits into the wallet at my belt because I wanted to buy the girl a ribbon if I were able to meet her once more and put the rest, carefully wrapped up in an old cloth to prevent it from jingling, into a small bag that I wore under my coat. It was midafternoon and I was about to scramble out of the hollow when I heard voices and a heavy, unexpected tramping of feet. I rammed the branches again hastily across the opening because I did not want to be discovered so near the sanctuary and peeped cautiously between the leaves.

The village priest was walking down the slope with a sickle in his hand, followed by about a dozen herdsmen. I started. Had I forgotten so much of my early training? This was the day for the blessing of the cattle.

They were already abreast of me but I was well hidden. Unfortunately there was a small clearing a few yards away and the priest paused there to pray before they left the trees. The villagers seemed awed and uncertain as they gathered in front of him; one coughed and almost choked himself trying to stop the sound, another looked terrified because a stick dropped from his old and almost useless fingers. I could not recognize the words and it was hard to remember as I watched the priest's fanatical gestures that he and my uncle belonged to the same faith. Honorius had prided himself upon his studies and his knowledge of Wales and Gaul. This man, I knew, resented the slightest change. The inner meaning of the words he said did not matter to him, he listened only for the augury if a word were accidentally slurred. All the same, a boy stepped forward with a bowl of milk to pour on the ground, precisely as I had taken one to Kaden or my uncle at how many similar occasions? The herdsmen prostrated themselves, the priest's voice rang out sharply and in the moment of silence before the worshippers began to scramble to their feet I heard a branch snap. A panting figure raced up the slope and stopped in front of them with uplifted hand.

I wondered if it were a difference in the ceremony and poked my head more out of cover than was wise when I recognized Lydd. The priest was in his robes, Lydd was caked with mud and was even without his badge yet a flash of recognition passed between them as if they were equals. Lydd moved his hand up and back with extended fingers for no apparent reason and as I was wondering what he was doing here a boyhood memory flashed into my mind. I had heard a yell on one of my uncle's visits to Godrevy and had rushed out to find Lydd, whom he had brought with him, wailing and rubbing his arm. "Do not try those tricks on me again," Honorius had said sternly and then, as he saw me watching them, he had ordered me as angrily to go back into the house. I had watched for an opportunity, begged a cake and taken it later to Lydd in one of the barns. "I was only trying to learn a sign or two," he had grumbled, "but he's jealous of his power."

"What signs?" I had asked and Lydd had explained that some of the priests were taught an old and secret language so that they could discuss matters of state at the great annual assemblies without even the kings' knowing what was said. Sometimes they used signs and sometimes ancient words. "It takes several years to learn them properly," he had grunted with his mouth full of cake, "but I have managed to pick up a greeting or two." I had admired his skill, I suppose I was about ten years old, and he had shown me a signal, it was a rune done with three fingers in the air, that the messengers used if they went to another court.

The priest was now looking at Lydd in utmost surprise while there was an expression of cunning and an almost frightening joy upon the exile's face. Lydd muttered a sentence or two; the elder took three steps forward, said the last prayer and blessed each herdsman as the man put his tribute into the basket carried by two boys. It was only after he had ordered these youths to go down to the village and they were completely alone that he turned to Lydd and said in plain and everyday language, "I have never heard so grave an accusation. Have you witnesses? How can you prove it?"

"He is to meet her again in two days."

"I cannot go to the King and tell him that his daughter

was sleeping with a common sailor while he was praying at the sanctuary without more proof than your mere word. If they were within the oaks, it will bring ruin to the harvest."

I stiffened in horror. Moram's daughter! Why had I not followed my first instinct and left the girl alone? It had been Lydd's head and no other that I had noticed between the trees and if they caught me now I should die more miserably than the Frisian. He had perished swiftly with a single dart through the throat, whereas if I were bound to a stake to suffer the "arrow death" they prided themselves upon the torment lasting an hour.

"No," Lydd shook his head, "there will be no famine. The girl was careful. The stream is the boundary so they were both outside."

I let go the branch in my hand. If we had not been within the "oak shadow" there was still a chance of escape. I was, and was not, innocent. Neither Osmund nor my comrades could save me but perhaps because I had thought of the Frisian, Friedowald's round, hairy face flashed into my mind. I had little to offer him but there was a chance that he might pity me, though only (I thought grimly) if he happened to be on good terms with the wind when I reached him. He was not twenty miles away by a straight road but the boundaries were watched by Moram's guards.

"Ask the King where he left his daughter," Lydd continued. "Ruan left us at dawn and is not yet here. I can walk, not run, the distance in three hours."

"He may have witnesses who saw him in the valley."

"No," Lydd laughed maliciously and, terrified as I was, I wondered at his hatred, "I was resting under a bank when he asked the way from a shepherd."

"I wonder the man sent a stranger along that track."

"Oh, I might have suggested it to him," Lydd answered with a grin, "I had noticed Ruan talking to the girl the previous evening." It was a lie, I had never seen her before and I crushed a stick with a snap in my fury. I thought that they must have heard it and prepared to spring at Lydd's throat but they were too absorbed, it seemed, to notice the sound or perhaps each thought the other had happened to step backwards on some twig.

"Even this is not proof," the priest said and, however much I had objected to his intolerance and pride during the winter, there was a magnificence in the way that even this fanatic upheld our laws although he would do nothing to mitigate their harshness. He would see that I had a hearing but what would it avail me? I had to reach Friedowald or I was lost.

"Then come with me in two days and we shall catch them together, or if the girl is alone we can make her confess." Lydd spoke as gaily as if he were inviting a friend to supper and not plotting the shame of the King and his daughter nor my own death.

"Very well, I will join you," the priest said reluctantly, "but meantime do not show yourself either at the King's hall or at the harbor. They may have been outside the boundary but wantonness in a king's family is an evil omen for our people. Perhaps it will teach our rulers to forbid the sailors landing here and bringing with them misery and change." He put his hand on Lydd's shoulder and in some strange way I wondered in the midst of my own danger whether this were not a healing for Kaden's fist? Had Lydd always been treacherous or had there been a moment when he might have followed the example of Honorius instead of that of his unknown, plundering father? They passed so close to my hiding place that I was surprised that they did not hear my heart beating or the grass rustling round my knees, and as they turned the corner I heard Lydd say triumphantly, "This is not the first time that Ruan has been in trouble. He was turned out of his uncle's home for disobedience. It was the reason why he went to sea."

It was an hour before sunset. Everything was quiet. Two women were carrying a basket of linen from the drying ground back to the huts. A dozen children were chasing each other in and out of the bushes, the village elders were chattering together in the shelter of a sunny bank. They had launched the *Seagull* during my absence but the water casks were still on the shore. A sailor was repainting the dragon on the bow, there were others busy at different points along the deck. I clenched my fists angrily and forgot my grumbles; my friends were there, my world, my happiness, why must I lose them all because of a single foolish act? My oar, my sleeping place, the stale water and the planklike bread were greater treasures to me at that moment than Friedowald's fables about islands full of gold. I would trust my comrades and tell

Osmund my story, they would not abandon me because I was in danger.

I began to stride down the path in full view of the village only to stop after I had taken half a dozen steps. Osmund had warned us to leave the native girls alone. Suppose, to save me, he set sail this very evening, we should lose most of our stores and if the priest cursed us it might bring disaster on our ship. Once Osmund knew the truth, even though I jumped off the cliff to escape being tortured, Moram could fine him heavily and he would never be able to winter in this part of Ireland again. No, it was my duty to try to reach Friedowald. They could not prove me guilty until they could confront me with the girl. If I did not return, Osmund could honestly say that Lydd's story was merely a tale to account for my disappearance but what chance had I of reaching the Finn's port?

It was not far and in the next King's territory, but who could cross the dense forests and the treacherous swamps that formed the boundary between the two kingdoms? There was a road but it was guarded and the messenger who had come to us in the spring had had to pay a heavy toll for the token that had permitted him to use it. A merchant who had joined him for part of the way had had to wait in a dirty hut at the post for almost a week before they had found him a guide. I looked at the sea; the last rays of sunlight warmed the backs of my hands, my full strength had come to me, I did not want to die. Darkness was near, I thought in despair, the actual blackness of the lonely night and an infinite density that rolled towards me like a fog. I remembered the sparks from the pyre on Agnas and my uncle's words, "There will be neither moon nor stars to light you on your way." What could I do? A hoe rasped on a stone. I looked round desperately and saw the surly slave that had waited on us at the feast, working in a field. Where had I heard that the man had once been a fowler's serf and knew the marshes better than Nera himself?

"Melvas," I called in a low sharp whisper, "come here."

He had been prodding the ground aimlessly and looked up with a scowl. I suppose that he expected me to scold him.

"You said the other day that you would rather die than spend another winter in Ireland."

A gleam of hope came into his eyes although he made no answer and his stubborn face might have been carved out of wood. His silence annoyed me and I continued angrily, "Listen, I am risking my life by asking you, but Lydd is my enemy, because of a supposed wrong that my uncle did him in childhood, and he is about to tell King Moram that I slept with his daughter in the woods. It's a foolish tale but I lost my way in the hills and cannot prove I was alone." I knew that if I told Melvas the truth he would be too frightened to help me.

"What has this to do with me?" Melvas grunted. "Your captain will protect you."

"The ship is not ready to sail, we should be held here till the best cargoes were lost and what can Osmund do

154

when I have no witnesses? Guide me through the marshes and I will pay your passage back to Wales."

"Yet you have served your captain faithfully," Melvas said, scratching his ear, as if we were exchanging riddles.

"I am not his chief steersman, he can easily replace me."

"It could not happen with us." Melvas stooped, pulled up a tuft of grass and began to clean the blade of his hoe. "Now when a stranger, not one of my own people, mind you, but a stranger, came to King . . ."

"Melvas, there is not a moment to lose. If you will guide me through that bog, I will give you this." I held up a double link of gold.

Melvas straightened himself and dropped the grass. "If they put the trackers on us they will chop my ears off, or perhaps a hand, for trying to escape." He looked at my face for reassurance and then down to the gold in my hand. "Will you come?" I asked for the second time.

"They can still seize me at the harbor. . . ."

"Not as long as you have your passage money on you. Besides, my friends will hide you until you can find a ship."

"How do I know that you will not kill me once you have crossed, so as not to have to give me the gold?"

It was simply a pretext to gain time while he turned things over in that somewhat too thick skull of his. "You are as strong as I am," I answered, "we will divide our weapons and I'll swear by your gods if you wish, as well as mine."

Melvas grubbed a weed out again with his hoe. I was afraid that a boy might notice us but I dared not be impatient. "I will take you," he said at last. "All you seamen are raiders but I think you will keep your bargain and Lydd had me whipped last year for losing an ax that was never in my hands. When will they discover your flight? We cannot cross the marshes in darkness."

I hesitated. The priest had wanted to wait until my supposed next meeting with the girl but I suspected that Lydd in his impatience would rush immediately to Moram with his story. Even so, he could not reach the King's hall until late at night and they would look for me first among my shipmates. "We have till noon tomorrow, perhaps some hours longer, provided that nobody has seen me here."

"Good!" It was extraordinary how something in Melvas seemed to come alive. He would swing an ax as well as any of us, I thought, looking at his broad shoulders, once he had had some training. "I shall go straight to the village and get some food and my cloak but meet me three fields above here at the first blink of light," he scratched the position rapidly on the earth in front of him, "and remember," he added, with a heavy attempt at a smile, "if you oversleep yourself I shall not wait for you." I smiled as I watched him running down the path because "as slow as Melvas" had become a proverb in the village. He stopped after a few paces, turned, and came back towards me with an anxious look in his eyes. "Show me the gold again," he begged. I held the links up while he gazed at them with the avid expression that I had noticed on Friedowald's face when he had got out his chart. "Have no fear," I tried to reassure him, "I swear that I will treat you as if you were my brother. We shall be back in Wales, if fortune is with us, before the next full moon."

I slept in my woodland hollow for the last time but I was at the meeting place well before dawn, as frightened as I had ever been in my life. I doubted that Melvas would betray me, otherwise the men and hounds would already be out on the hills, but there were plenty of dangers apart from any pursuit, we could lose ourselves or run into a tracker on his ordinary round. Every time that a tiny animal rustled through the brambles, my hand flew to my knife, I heard footsteps but nothing was there and by the time that Melvas came panting up the hill I was almost ready to run to the village and give myself up. "I had to wait until they let out the cows," he explained, "but I did not waste my time. I knew where the cook had hidden some meat and I have got a joint and two loaves."

"Get your breath while we fasten up your things." We divided the food and it was only after I had helped him roll his cloak and sling it with his bag over his shoulder that I ventured to ask him, "Which way do we go?"

"First we climb the hill. We follow the ridge for a while until we can drop to the next valley, then it's swamps until we get to the forest. It is so bad in places that there is no fixed boundary. I've known that bog swallow up a pony. It's not a spot to be crossed in a hurry."

I had expected to be faster than Melvas, but once we

started, his slow lumbering strides covered the ground as quickly as my own steps. The turf was wet with dew, the air was fresh, it was like any one of a hundred such mornings when I had driven the flocks to pasture as a boy. If they did not fade, if it were only color that counted, the gorse flowers were a brighter gold than the links in my bag. Birds sang as we climbed steadily upwards and as we came to the summit after a march of two hours it seemed impossible not to be alive when everything was growing and new. I turned to look for a last time at our ship. She was riding as easily as the gulls after which she was named on the smooth, blue water. It was too early for my shipmates to be aboard but there was our broken barrel sticking out of the sand, an oar (or was it a strip of wood?) was still lying on the pebbles and was that squat, slightly bent figure our steersman, picking his way across the beach? The village was further inland, it was hard to distinguish the dirty hut of our long, grumbling winter from its fellows but I could see the chief's hall and the flat space where the Frisian had died. The white, withered flower that the Irish girl had given me was still sticking to my coat. I ripped it off and flung it angrily away. I was tempted to retrace my steps. What could Friedowald offer me if I found him but a useless voyage through a waste of ice where the winds would cut our bare flesh like a sword? Surely Osmund would protect me? Why should I obliterate the fellowship of years with this unnecessary flight? "Hurry," Melvas plucked me by the sleeve, he must have read my thoughts. "There will be no pity for either of us if Moram's guards find us and I never want to see that harbor again as long as I live."

What was the old saying? Not every man can eat his brother's meat. My memories were of friendship and warmth; to Melvas, the village was a place of punishment and despair. I had to put my homesickness behind me, my duty now was to this dark-haired Welshman whom I had tempted into such danger. Fate seemed to be with us for the moment, we raced across the bare top of the hill and down the path that ended near the bog without meeting a shepherd or even a stray hound. "I have been uneasy ever since we landed," I panted, "Lydd met me the day I came ashore and I have felt all winter long that something was going to happen."

Melvas stopped; he lifted a frond of bracken and, reading some sign from it that I could not understand, turned to the right. In a short time we were jumping from one hummock to another across ground that, though green, was already half water. "If you have a feud with the man you must have done him some injury," he said, as if my words had just reached his ears.

"No real injury," I assured him but I saw that Melvas did not believe me. "Lydd could not forgive my uncle for saving his life as a child." There was more truth in an old woman's saying than men would admit. I had heard my grandmother whisper, when I was a child, that if a maid were ravished against her will, her child would be deformed in mind or body. Yet I, myself, had slept with the Irish girl although it was true that she had been the first to call me from my way. Lydd, myself, which of us was to blame? It was as complicated as any spider's web, shimmering among the rafters.

"It is right for a man to accept the consequences of his kinsman's acts," Melvas continued, as if he were preaching a sermon, "we cannot escape our sins."

"It was no sin, my uncle treated him like a son," I protested hotly and yet, though it was strange at this moment to be making excuses for an enemy, I remembered how the boys had made fun of the dirty, awkward child. "Beggar's foundling," they had called him, when my uncle was out of earshot. At first Lydd had fought them and afterwards, because he was slighter and much younger, he had twisted the term into an excuse for his own faults and wantonness. How our actions linked themselves one into the other and yet why had Lydd turned against Honorius, who had been kind to him, instead of against his tormentors?

"I envied no man his hall," Melvas said bitterly, "I was content to herd my father's cows. Then you sailors stole me away."

"The gods will our lives, not men," I answered, and we strode on in silence although I should have stopped to admire the beauty of the landscape if the terror of the "arrow death" had not hung over us. The grass was short and green and soft as some enormous flower. It was still early enough for the water to run smoothly through the marsh lilies. They were not yet out, but in another week the channels would appear to swarm with butterflies as the yellow spikes opened, clump by clump. Every now and then I jumped across a tuft of tiny white blossoms almost as much in his boat as in the hut and he would have let me escape, only he knew that I should be recognized as a runaway unless I had money and other clothes. I meant to try, all the same, but he died quite suddenly and while I was burying him some hunters came and took me back to the King. He sold me to Bresal and Bresal put me to work on his fields."

It was easy to see how these swamps guarded a country better than fortifications. The pools were deep enough to drown a man if he stumbled in the dark and the tangled growth of submerged and sticky weeds caught a buckle or in the hem of his cloak. A few weeks before the water would have frozen round our leggings; in summer the place would be black with flies. Yet Melvas stopped to pick a fragrant leaf and gave me a second one to chew. "If I get home," he said, "this is the only place I shall remember. I like the herons rising at sunset for their last kill and the big green frogs, leaping from leaf to leaf. I lifted one up once in my hand, it was all fear and a big thumping heart."

This was one of the strangest days in my life; in spite of Lydd, we were both so happy. We had neither to pull nor dig and we were far from the stench of offal pits in this remote, deserted valley. I should have liked to linger and watch the moor hens rise above the streams that crossed and recrossed each other in the aimless way we children had scratched marks on oyster shells, calling em our charts, or to pause for a moment to scrunch re water mint and get my breath but Melvas strode that we called bonewort and the Irish wood violets. My mother had pounded the roots and mixed them with spring water. They comforted an anxious heart. The water birds rose angrily from the rushes as we splashed past, the air was as soft as a king's linen shift. How strange it was to think that Lydd was running through almost as lovely a landscape in the opposite direction to bring about our death! I wondered again why he hated me so much. "It is the bending of the twig that the tree never forgives," I said, almost imitating my uncle's voice, then I stepped into a hole that I had not noticed and clutched wildly at my companion's shoulder.

Melvas looked round. "You have to be careful in these bogs," he grunted, adding as we came to firmer ground, "The bracken comes back when you take our oxen from us and then whole villages starve." There was another splash before I could answer and this time Melvas sank up to his knees in mud. He shook himself, scratched his head and moved cautiously to the left. "How did you learn the way?" I asked, knowing that I could never ha crossed the quagmire alone, every reed and leaf and mock seemed alike to me.

"I was sold to King Moram with some othe as soon as we were landed. Nobody could und tongue and I would not learn theirs, so aft for a month, the King sent me to one of man needed help to build a new cora hut up that hill, it's about three m fowler was an old man and did no if he should die, so he taught steadily on until we saw the forest, a little way to our right, after we had been walking about eleven hours.

"We have to climb here," Melvas said, "and quickly, because we must get across the open ground before nightfall. There should be a swineherd's hut about a mile away. The fowler took me there once to get a jar of honey. He gave the man two ducks for it. . . ." Melvas looked up at me, expecting me to be astonished but I answered indifferently, "You must have had excellent hunting."

"But ducks are not for swineherds," Melvas continued in a shocked voice. "A messenger usually came to collect the birds and bring us bread, but that week he was late. The man showed us where he led his swine into the woods to get acorns but I shall never find the spot if it is dark."

I looked back at the marshes. How beautiful they were, with the evening light shimmering on the water, the floating leaves, and the almost yellow stems of what we called the wattle rush. The lethargy that I had felt during the winter months had gone. I wanted to live. A panic seized me; I started to bound up the slope. "Wait," Melvas shouted, "there is nobody after us yet," and as he caught up with me he took hold of my belt. Then we climbed, steadily but at an even pace, until we reached the top of the ridge and saw the trees in front of us.

The forest was dark and dangerous. It was full of owls, wild cats, outlaws and, some said, magic. A fugitive who tried to find his way through it alone usually disappeared. The advantage of approaching it by way of the swamps was that the edge above them was left unguarded; the solitary road passed near the center and was always watched.

How deserted it was and lonely. I had often felt in Cornwall that the rocks brooded over the passers-by but here the land was calm; foals, men and thistledown were all one to it. Melvas walked slowly, looking from side to side, then he clutched my elbow with a joyful shout. "It's there!" he said, pointing to an oak. "The swineherd told us to look for a tree that had lost two branches on one side, it should be quite a good path."

We sat down for a moment to eat some food and scrape the worst of the mud from our leggings. It had been a long march, we had not come far in actual distance but we had waded part of the way knee-deep in water and we were both tired. I rerolled my cloak, took a final jab at my boots with the end of a bent twig and stared despondently at the landscape. At about this hour, my comrades would be strolling up from the beach and I knew how sweet the scent of gorse and pasture seemed in the last days before sailing. How I dreaded having to join a new, and possibly unfriendly, crew where I should have to learn the positions of the ropes again instead of feeling instinctively for them. At that moment Melvas clutched my arm, "They know!" He sprang up in such terror that he dropped both knife and meat to the ground. Two thin spirals of smoke—this was the warning signal —rose into the air from the crest of the hill that we had climbed early that morning. "Lydd went straight to the King," I said; it was exactly what I had feared.

Melvas picked up his knife, we grabbed our bundles and raced into the forest. It was probable that they would look first for us along the road but as an outlaw might win a pardon if he delivered us up to our pursuers, dead or alive, we might hear the whistle of an arrow at any moment. The track had been little used but it was still visible and it was easier to push through the under-growth than we had expected. There were obstacles: we had to make a half circle round a huge, fallen elm but a certain amount of light reached us through the branches that were not yet in full leaf. We stooped under matted twigs, jumped from one moss-covered boulder to an-other, and stood still if a dry bush rustled against our leggings. It was not yet time for either cats or owls to hunt and for the moment speed was more essential than silence. First Melvas went in front and I followed about ten paces behind him so that if beast or enemy sprang from a bough I could shout a warning and go to his help; then, after he was exhausted, I took his place, and we made good progress until the increasing darkness made it impossible to see a yard in front of us. We judged that we must be halfway across.

"Your swineherd's path seems to lead straight to the other side," I whispered. "Of course, he brought the pigs in for the acorns but no doubt a couple of peddlers followed him. Some of the tales we have heard must have been spread deliberately to make sure your friend got a reward for showing them the way." Fate must have heard me make this foolish remark because as I uttered it the track branched to the right. We should have tried to climb a tree to get some direction from the stars or else have forced a way forward through the ground ivy and ferns. We lost our wits instead and kept to the same path, because we were tired and it was easy, only to have it end at a deep pool when it was too dark to retrace our steps.

We were trapped. The bushes grew densely round the water and though Melvas discovered what he thought was an opening it was only the run that some wild cat had made. We followed it all the same for a few moments until we were halted by a thicket of brambles and had to retrace our steps through sharp thorns and over roots that we could not see, as far as the pond. "At least they cannot find us here," I muttered but Melvas answered in an indignant whisper, "A man like Nera can follow our tracks as easily as if we had walked all this way across mud with our soles studded with nails."

We moved away from the water into the middle of some bushes because, however dangerous our position might be, we had to wait for dawn. We were so exhausted that I even slept for a time. I was wakened by Melvas shaking me by the shoulder. "Listen!" he whispered and I could feel his whole body trembling. "The hounds are out."

I sat up yawning, there was a bit of grass at the back of my collar and I wanted to scratch myself, then I too heard the baying of the animals and sprang to my feet. So Moram's men could really see in the dark or were they merely following the trained noses of their animals? I gazed at the clearing. Was this where hope and memory were to end, and the small skills that I had learned with

166

so much pain? Melvas would never see his father again and if I had not tempted him he would still be sleeping safely in his master's hut. I tried to fasten my belt that a branch had ripped and felt, a little foolishly, that I should have no time to mend it. "What can we do?" Melvas croaked, too shivering and frightened to move while the forest round us seemed to be full of noises. I looked up; a shaft of moonlight fell on a doe that had come to drink at the pool, she heard the hounds, her ears quivered and she sprang into the undergrowth. A gust of anger seemed to sweep through my head and in one of those instinctive flashes that sometimes save a life I splashed through the water as far as the spot where the deer had vanished and turned there as if to meet our pursuers. "Come!" I said sharply but with confidence. We broke through the brambles for a few yards and then, as if it were a path that I had often travelled or the reverse side of the Gaulish cup that I had not been allowed to lift, we jumped across a stump onto a narrow, twisting track that must have been made by the charcoal burners because there was an old, abandoned basket lying near the ashes of a fire. It swept round in the right direction, the hounds were nearer but we could run without brambles catching in our clothes. "They will lose the scent at the water," Melvas panted, "but not for long."

The trees thinned, a little light was coming into the sky; in spite of having followed the wrong road, we must be further across the forest than we had supposed. We ran until we had to slow down to a walk, ran again as soon as our breath came back to us, a moment came when we could hear the baying no longer and we raced at last on to a patch of grass and saw an open countryside in front of us.

I still held my broken strap in my hand. I would mend it tomorrow, I thought, as we dropped in sheer exhaustion under the nearest bank and, with no more than a grunt of thankfulness, went to sleep.

It was full morning when Melvas woke me. We were stiff, dirty and ravenous but though we shook the food sack over a rag there was barely a crumb left. Still, our luck had held. There were some ships in the bay and we decided that the one anchored nearest to the harbor was broad enough to be the *Walrus*.

I turned my back while Melvas was rolling up his cloak so that he could not see me fumble in my bag. "Here is your reward," I said, offering him three links of the gold that my uncle had once given me, "I have added an extra piece for good measure. Hide it, it may buy you some sheep when you get home." Melvas almost snatched the links and rubbed them between his fingers as if he feared that they were polished stones. "Come," I said impatiently because we should be in danger until we were at sea, "if they are short of men they may find you a place on the rowing benches and then you will have even enough to buy cows."

We strapped our gear about us for the last time while I glanced round gratefully at the bleak spot where we had slept. The grass was short, there was not a single spike of gorse, but it was outside Moram's territory and I could see smoke rising from the huts grouped round the port. "It was the pool," Melvas said, as if he were going over every step that we had taken in his mind. "How did you know that there was a path beyond that stump? I could see nothing but thorns."

"It was chance." Yet was it? The Gaulish artist could never have stumbled through the Irish bogs. I had not been inside the forest, so why should I have turned in the only direction in which escape was possible unless Fate had willed it? There was no apparent order in life. Why had Melvas been captured, Honorius dismissed after a lifetime of service, the Frisian killed on account of a drunken joke? The priests did not know the answers. They were as confused as we were and full of hatred for those who used different symbols from their own. Perhaps the world was old, so old that the men who might have taught us something had died, in a raid perhaps, or because nobody wanted their wisdom? I should always try to find the reason for the pattern but as I followed Melvas, who was several paces ahead of me, an overmastering fear drove all other questions out of my mind. Suppose Friedowald had sailed or could not take us, what should we do? Moram's band would keep within their territory but if their leader offered the headman at the harbor some small bribe, it was probable that he would surrender us. We were ragged and helpless strangers, who were unlikely to have relatives to pay a ransom. It took us about an hour to reach the village. There were nets drying over a frame, cracked barrels and a moldering heap of seaweed in front of the largest hut. A woman looked at us curiously but did not speak, and when a child pushed through the skins hanging over a door, the sudden smell of newly baked bread almost sent my hand to my bag for one of my few coins. It was a busy place, not unlike Godrevy, yet even if we wintered here we could never be a part of it. It was Melvas who saw the *Walrus* first as we dragged ourselves wearily towards the harbor. She was lying at anchor, as fat as a duck, glistening with new paint.

"Wait for me a moment," I begged as we came in front of a tumble-down hut that was apparently used for storing bait. I wanted to speak to Friedowald first alone.

Melvas nodded. He was about to drop onto a seat made by an upturned cask when he stopped and came back to me. I was about to assure him again that I would not desert him but he spoke first. "Here or in Wales, half of what I have is yours," he stammered and he meant it, at least for the moment, yet I knew that there was the wide sea between us as I thanked him. He was a landsman and the deep companionship of the last day and night would vanish before we made port, as Erbin and my other shipmates had gone, until their features and the sound of their voices were as shadowy as his separate voyages in an old man's head. We cannot keep our treasures, be they love, moments or memories, they fade, they dissolve as into the ruins of a sunset until, if the gods wish to bless us, they take us with them.

They had built a wall to keep the waves from nibbling away the land and there I found Friedowald sitting on top of a mooring post and bargaining with a merchant over a coil of rope. His back was towards me and I waited patiently until the trader turned to call his servant, then I crept forward, flung myself as a suppliant before him and seized his foot, "Have pity on me, Friedowald, I am in great danger."

"And I am buying timber." The Finn looked round at me in amazement. We had tried to clean ourselves but my leggings were coated with mud and I had not been able to pick all the burrs and threads of grass from my cloak. "Give us a place on your ship. Unless the gods had been with us, we should never have crossed the forest alive."

"Not so fast, Ruan, not so fast. Tell me first what has happened."

"It was Lydd, that fellow with the missing teeth who teased Nera until he fought the Frisian."

"Had you a feud with him?"

"No, it's a long story, he hated my uncle but without reason."

"There is always a reason. Did you fight with him?"

"He saw me sleeping with King Moram's daughter," I faltered, "it was spring."

"You what? You slept with the King's daughter? Are you out of your wits?" At first the Finn stared at me in astonishment, then he began to laugh, he roared until the tears poured out of his eyes and he had to cling to the mooring post with both hands.

"She told me that she was a serving maid. I found her in a wood."

"It is always dangerous to lie with a girl in the open, you may get an ague."

"I did," I said meekly, "but now we are in great danger. They chased us with hounds."

"Us? Who is with you?"

"Do you remember Melvas, that surly slave who poured our ale at the feast? He knew a secret path through the bog. They would have caught me otherwise and tortured me. I promised that I would help him return to his kindred in Wales."

"Quite the chief with retainers of your own," Friedowald sneered. "I am merely a seafarer, trying to get an ancient boat shipworthy enough to sail. I have nothing against any man sleeping with a woman on a winter night, if he so wishes, but in spring, when the voyages begin, the carelessness of it!"

I waited anxiously but the trader returned at that moment and Friedowald turned crossly away. "You will have to wait until I finish my business," he growled, "if the hounds reach you first, the ocean is below you."

It was cold comfort with the wind blowing through my still damp clothes. Everything seemed flat and stale. There were two different currents warring in my mind: I was thankful to have reached the harbor but whenever I noticed the *Walrus* I was lonely for my comrades and my own ship. There was a groove that my shoe had worn, forward from my bench. It had taken the shape of a favorite cliff and I had kept it free from water and dirt. What would it mean to whoever took my oar? He would no more notice the crack than he would know that if he caught them in an exact line between Osmund's shoulder and the center of the mast at the top of a roll, our figurehead's wings appeared to open and to be about to fly. I yawned, I was more battered than I had been after a three-day storm, yet in spite of my exhaustion I had to admire the skill with which Friedowald bartered a tattered sail for a perfectly solid plank. He had a gift that drew all sailors to him although he wore no outward sign of leadership but sat there in a skin coat that was covered with bare, rubbed patches, looking as old as his boat. It must have been half an hour before he looked up while the men were carrying away the sail. "Still so stupid, Ruan? It is gold and silver that count with me. If you want to be rescued, where is your passage money?"

I handed him my bag. I had taken the precaution to stuff one link into my leggings but he took the other and the little silver that remained, although I needed clothes, having lost my possessions. "And you think these are enough for a passage to Wales?" he said indignantly, as if I had offered him a handful of shells. I hesitated, other captains would have taken me for pity or for a quarter of what I offered but I was in the Finn's power; then I answered with a flash of inspiration, "You are sure of men to sail with you to Wales but how many of them will follow you afterwards? I offer you loyalty and I believe in your chart."

"I can buy the one and I do not need the other. Still, it would be a pity to see you wriggling full of darts when you might be swabbing my decks. You can come with me, I am just going aboard."

"Not without Melvas," I said stubbornly, "if it had not been for him I should have been drowned."

I thought that he was going to refuse and suddenly it seemed unimportant, all that I wanted was to get out of the wind and sleep. Then, as sometimes happened with Friedowald, he began to laugh. "I like to see a man loyal to his companions but find that fellow of yours quickly. There is a lot to be done on the *Walrus* and I want to sail before the first light."

I ran back, whistling. Melvas did not answer, he was not at the hut where I had left him and for one terrible moment I feared that some villager had seized him and taken him off to the headman's hearth. "Melvas!" I shouted more loudly than was wise. "Melvas!" I looked round, Friedowald was starting down the steps. "Melvas!" I could not bear any more, I was tempted to run back to the wharf and leave him to his fate but somehow, screaming his name as I moved, I looked inside the shelter again and there he was, sound asleep, with his ragged coat so much the color of the dirty, broken baskets all round him that if I had not stumbled over his leg I might never have seen him. "Wake up, the ship is sailing without us," I yelled. He struggled to his feet, then he realized what I was saying, started to run and was the first to reach the quay. Friedowald and his man were already in their scow and watching our frantic race with amusement. "Careful, careful," he growled as we scrambled aboard, "I've got a new length of rope on my lap and I don't want to get it wet. I see you need food," he added, looking with more sympathy at our hungry faces, "and perhaps some of the crew can lend you both dry cloaks."

There was more movement in the waves between us and the shore than I should have thought possible on so fine a summer day. They slapped against the sides of the *Walrus* and swung us round slowly so that I was looking first at one side of the anchorage and then at the other. I let the rope that I was supposed to be mending drop to my knees and watched the scene lazily as we moved. Low hill followed low hill on the nearer side with the road to the next town winding up the valley. I counted eleven sheep on the opposite slope but for a long time I could not find their shepherd; then I discovered him lying under a rock with his crook beside him, asleep, no doubt, in the sun.

We had had a quick passage from Ireland rather than a happy one. The crew did not know the ship and we had got in each other's way. Besides, after the first evening, nobody had wanted to hear our story; the escape had marked us for life but what did our dangers and hardships mean to strangers? I had also picked up an ague in the swamp that was still crawling about my bones. Melvas had grumbled the whole journey. He had never sat down to a meal without saying something that had spoilt our laughter: the water stank or he had found maggots in the bread, the piece of drifting timber was a sign that raiders were about and couldn't we feel that the wind was changing and that we should soon be becalmed? We had known that it was fear; with every hour that we had sailed closer to Wales his body had become so responsive to imaginary perils lest he should not reach home that he was almost out of his wits. It had been Friedowald of all of us who had understood him best; he had talked to him gently throughout the voyage and had taken him ashore directly we had anchored while Melvas had shouted farewell to me from the coracle as if I had been a passing acquaintance rather than his companion.

Destiny had a passion, I thought, for treating mankind as children treat the shells they scatter haphazardly around them after a morning on the beach. It was useless now to turn my life over in my mind, there was no straight line, it wandered, lost itself in something perilously like our swamps, doubled back, went forward and arrived eventually at a point that was different from my original goal. It was useless dreaming about Godrevy now, if wandering were in a man the urge was in him till he died and I knew that if I hired myself to some farmer on land my palms would itch for an oar and the growl of a shipmate taking soundings as soon as the new lambs were in the fold and the gorse came into flower again. I did not want to go back to the trading fleet, I was satiated with its familiar dangers. Yet what was the truth behind Friedowald's chart and were we really equipped for so long and dangerous a journey? We needed fresh water barrels and another pair of sails. He was not a miser when it came to his ship but unless he could get a very good price for the hides that we had just unloaded he would have to go back to Ireland for more cargo and I should have to find another captain.

The gentle, rocking movement must have lulled me to sleep because I was suddenly startled by Friedowald's voice behind me. "I thought so! Dozing, instead of mending my rope, but we had a hard day yesterday with those bales. You can come ashore with me if you like and look for a better coat, that thing you are wearing isn't even a shirt, it's a net."

It was not far to the shore and the tide was with us but as I glanced up at the line of soft, green hills stretching into the distance I still wondered if I should not leave the ship and try a summer ashore? I had had enough of danger and, although I knew that I had never sailed with so experienced a captain, I mistrusted Friedowald's island. It was one thing to talk about it over the ale at a feast and another to set out across an unknown ocean with so inadequate a chart. There would be plenty of food on a farm and, although I liked neither chopping wood nor herding cattle, there was always a chance that Osmund might drop anchor in the harbor. I had been here with him once although the Brittany fleet, as a rule, assembled further south.

Friedowald did not speak until we landed, then he put his hand into his wallet and drew out some pieces that I recognized as the silver that I had given him. "Get yourself some clothes," he grunted, "but bargain for them properly. Be sure not to give the man the first price he asks."

I would have refused the money had I dared because I resented the Finn's assumption that I was some fool on his first voyage. Yet I had to get a sleeping fleece and though I had worn my best coat when I had gone to see

Moram, it was scuffed and dirty and my footgear was worn out. "It's your due," he added, seeing my hesitation, "you worked your passage and even your friend was a better scrubber than he thought." He thrust the bits into my hand and I thought with some bitterness that he had kept the gold link for himself. "You have till nightfall," he added and then, while I was busy with the coracle, he waddled with the short, important steps of a puffin towards the solitary inn.

There were only a couple of farms, a smith's forge, and a few other buildings by the shore but I had no trouble in buying the things that I needed because few sailors had the time to walk into the actual town. It was built for safety several miles inland. I even got a new jacket, it was not as good as the one I had but it was clean. The seller told me that Melvas had found his father, the old man had moved to a valley miles away behind a range of hills. "He came here twice," the man said helping me to strap my purchases together inside a fleece, "he wanted to ask the captains about ransoming his son but nobody could find out where the boy was."

I felt hurt for a moment that Melvas had sent me no message but then I remembered that I had refused all his offers to leave the *Walrus* and go to his home. Four or five women had brought their children to the sands; they were sitting in a circle carding wool and laughing as they worked. A girl was dabbling her feet in the water, two little boys were turning the stones over to see if they could find a crab, but I felt discontented and trapped; the effort of the flight seemed to have drained me of my

178

strength and there was enough swamp fever left to chill my bones. I still had an hour to spare and was wandering aimlessly between the booths when I almost bumped into a gray-haired man who came striding down one of the side lanes. We looked at each other carelessly then recognition came to us both at the same moment. "Dungarth!" I cried joyfully, "Oh, Dungarth! It's good to see you."

He was the same sunburnt figure that had taken me fishing as a boy though his cheeks were more wrinkled and his shoulders were a little bent. I must have changed even more because it was a moment or two before he said, "Why, Ruan, I never expected to see you again. I thought you had either gone to Ireland or were drowned."

"I was three years with the trading fleet to Brittany, now I'm on the *Walrus*, that first boat there in the anchorage."

"So it's Ruan, Ruan . . ." he repeated my name slowly as if he were not altogether pleased about the meeting.

"Come and eat," I suggested, "the sun will set in a moment and I have so much to ask you."

It was a small village and the only inn was a few paces away. It was a cheerful place and as we walked through the doorway I saw Friedowald sitting opposite a merchant in one corner of the room. I settled Dungarth first in front of a table and then went over to the Finn. "Give me leave to spend the evening ashore," I asked him, cap in hand, "I have just met a kinsman from my village."

Friedowald looked first at me and then across at Dungarth. "A captain, I see," he said sharply and it was only

179

much later that I discovered that he supposed that I was trying to transfer to another ship. "You may do as you please provided that you are on board at sunrise to help unload the rest of the hides. You will have to borrow a coracle somewhere if I have left." Then he turned his back to me and went on talking to the trader.

"There is so much I want to know," I said, after I had rejoined Dungarth and a woman had brought us bread, ale and some strips of the famous dried mutton from the Welsh hills. "Are you here with your ship? Have you been back to the islands and what really happened to my uncle?"

"Why did you run away?" Dungarth replied in his turn. "Your uncle needed you those last few months."

"I should have fought with our supplanters if I had gone back. It would only have made things worse."

"I told him as much. I always said that you would have been better on my ship but he would not listen to me."

"That was what Lydd said too," and I wondered as I broke off a bit of meat if Lydd had really escaped into the woods and if I should ever know his fate.

"Lydd? But you hardly saw that scoundrel when you were young."

"I met him afterwards," I explained but I was not going to tell Dungarth about my own adventures until I had heard his news. "Is it true that my uncle received a chain of gold and died at my brother's house?"

"Yes." Dungarth's restless fingers kept tracing the pattern of the wood in front of him as if he wanted to make the table into a spar. "Nobody harmed him but the sickness came back with the first winter days and he died at the turn of the year."

"Did he speak of me?"

"Not at first. You made him very angry and he even suspected me of hiding you but then he said, it must have been the last time that I saw him, 'Ruan was a willful boy but perhaps it was for the best.' He was always fond of you."

"And my brother?"

"Growing fat. He joined the King's party as soon as your uncle died. Never go back to Godrevy, Ruan, if you value your freedom."

The innkeeper's wife entered with a dish of freshly cooked mackerel and another loaf. Dungarth was silent till he had finished his portion. "It's good to taste fish again," he said finally, wiping his mouth, "we get good meat in the hills but this makes a change."

"In the hills? Have you left the sea?"

"The King gave command of my ship to another man, my wife died shortly afterwards and so I came here with a couple of friends."

"He took the ship from you?"

"Yes and I got no gold chain." Dungarth smiled and called for another jug of ale. "Still, I was able to sell my house for a reasonable sum and I had always saved something from my voyages. I'm a farmer now, you must come and see me."

"And the islands?" I asked the question that had been uppermost in my mind while all the scenes of my boyhood, the golden bobbles on the thong weed in the Sound or the wolflike spring of the foam on a stormy day, tumbled into my mind to haunt me. "Did the King try to seize them?"

"No, he left them to starve. But your uncle gave me some links of gold before he died and I took my kinsman's boat across with a cargo of grain and timber. Their seer had already warned them that there would be changes. They bought my cargo so I did not lose on the voyage."

"But now?" I asked anxiously. "How can they live without grain?"

Dungarth looked me up and down and grinned, "You're my cousin, Ruan, and I will tell you the truth. I took over as much timber as wheat and we built a ship. They cross once a summer now themselves, not to Belerion but up north. I taught some of the men, your Erbin among them, all I could about our rocks."

"I want to go back to them," I said.

"Give them another few years. Their seer has said that any stranger other than myself might bring destruction on them, but he will not live forever and then there will be changes. The men like the annual voyage and hearing news in the market. I told your Erbin that you had run away, he was horrified at your disobedience at first but I think that he was glad afterwards to hear that you were a sailor."

"You never wanted to join the King's party yourself?" I asked out of curiosity, knowing what it must have cost Dungarth to give up command of his ship.

"I never pretended to be a priest like your uncle, Ruan,

but suppose I had abandoned the faith in which I was brought up for the sake of power, I should not have prospered. It would have been the first step to selling a bit of the cargo for myself or neglecting the helm."

I nodded, people seemed more greedy now and less honest than in my boyhood. "There have to be changes," Dungarth continued, "but I leave them to the young. When we understand, we have grown too old to feel."

"But are you happy here?" I asked.

"It was hard at first but yes, now I am content. I like listening to the winds with a roof over my head. Besides, a man from my ship came with me and I have a neighbor, who do you think he is?"

I shook my head.

"Your friend Kaden."

"Kaden!"

"Adversity has made him human. He still teaches your uncle's doctrine to a couple of boys but he is very interested in my bees when he comes over to taste their honey. It's not our own land but I think we are growing roots."

"Did my uncle say anything else about me?" I begged because I could see that Dungarth was getting drowsy.

"He was not angry with you, Ruan, set your mind at rest, not after he had left the Court and come to live at Godrevy. He told your brother that the sea was in your blood and that you were to be welcomed if you ever returned to the village. Strangely enough, he worried about Lydd. The last words he said to me before I left him were, 'I failed that boy. Lydd needed me more than Ruan.'"

"Lydd! Nobody could fail Lydd," I said contempt-uously, thinking of the baying of the hounds at the clearing in the forest, but I was too tired myself to begin the story of my Irish adventures. Yet as if some faint memory of youth had drawn me there, I smelt the thyme bushes in Dungarth's former garden above the heap of our discarded fish bones and the ale; I lived again through that July night. My former existence split like the husk of a nut, the guilt that had oppressed me through so many sorrowful watches dissolved as I watched Dungarth's head sink sleepily forward onto his arms; now, and not five years previously, my real life was to begin. It might bring happiness, it might bring death, it would be quite new. I got up quietly, took my coat and paid the inn-keeper, nobody followed me as I strolled into the street, I feared no cries. There was only the scent of camomile in the air as there had been then and the sighing of a wave rushing to silence along the coast.

To my surprise, because Friedowald had left the inn earlier than we had, our coracle was still drawn up on the beach. It could have been Godrevy cove, the same dark sea washed up the pebbles and further back the familiar clumps of heather almost covered a couple of stones. I had only been there a few moments when the Finn came striding down the sand. "So early?" he mocked. "I thought you were staying with your kinsman till dawn?"

"He went to sleep."

"I noticed he was an old man. Which is his ship?"

"He has left the sea. He told me about my home but

he was obliged to leave and he has warned me never to return there."

"You can join your friend Melvas. Thanks to you, his parents had to pay no ransom and they will treat you like a son."

I could smell the yellow and white stars of camomile in the pasture and inland I should have to face neither a nor'easter sweeping through my salt-soaked clothes nor an ocean for which there was no chart. I was opening my mouth to explain this to the Finn when I heard a surge of water in my ears that ebbed and thundered again and through it, like the final word of a tale, a voice said, "Ask." I turned, I knew that Friedowald would never believe me but it was true. He was inspecting a dent in the hide of the coracle as if it were of far more importance than a mere sailor and I had to tap him on the shoulder before he looked at me. "I am your man," I said, "I should have no happiness if I were to break my oath." I had not actually sworn myself to Friedowald and I still did not know if he meant to include me in his crew but he had rescued us from Ireland and for this voyage at least I had to follow him.

"Go to Melvas freely," Friedowald said with a smile, "I am not as greedy as you think."

"I am your man," I repeated in a quiet voice.

"Go to Melvas, Ruan, he is offering you a home."

"I can't," I said triumphantly, "I heard the singing."

"You heard what?"

"The singing. You told me that we heard it if we were summoned."

185

"A sailor, yes, but what are you, I wonder? You can pull a scow and scrub down a plank but you can't tell me when the wind is going to change."

"You must not blame me," I said boldly, "for not having been born a Finn."

"So you thought you heard the summons," the walrus head nodded maliciously. "Do you know what happened? While you were sleeping instead of mending my ropes, some water splashed into your ears."

"I am going with you," I said, it is true without much firmness because a roof and a fire were good on a stormy day.

Friedowald looked me up and down as if I were a flea-bitten hound. "Nobody seems to know where that Breton fellow I wanted is, so I suppose you can come as second steersman if you want. No, do not thank me, the Breton would have been more useful. Now I shall have to do most of the work myself. And don't stand lingering about this beach but push the coracle off. Time is short and I want to get some sleep."

The great seas had subsided, the wind came from the right quarter but it was as cold as an autumn day. Friedowald was sitting on an upturned barrel at the stern of the boat. His gray cloak was wound so tightly about him that he looked like one of the stone lookouts that the Welsh had begun to build along the coast. "Our course is right," he said with a worried expression, "but why are there so many gulls? It's a week since we last saw land."

"It's not as if there were much for them to eat," I answered mournfully as the cook flung a meager pail of scraps over the side. Friedowald had ordered the food to be halved that was served to us at a meal although we had plenty on board and the sharp air made us hungry.

"Must you always think of your belly?" Friedowald grumbled. "I do not want to use up all our stores."

I nodded, the waves dipped and rose, rose and dipped again like a herd of the sturdy ponies that ran half wild on the Welsh hills but I felt that I could face the future better with some meat or even a bowl of porridge inside me.

"I could have filled up the gaps in the crew," Friedo-wald continued almost as if he were asking for my confidence, "but it would have meant taking strangers and they might have been outlaws. If you ship a man with a blood feud on his hands, he is likely to be troublesome."

"Or worse," I agreed. It was not unknown for such men to seize the ship and go off raiding after throwing the master overboard. We should be short-handed if we ran into a gale but it was still a week to Midsummer Eve and we ought to have another two months of fair weather in front of us.

"Are you regretting you came?" the Finn asked so anxiously that I wondered if he wanted some reassurance himself.

"No," I shook my head, "no other course was open to me."

"Peril is a good teacher," the broad face wrinkled into a grin, "you would now be on a quiet voyage to Brittany if you had kept away from the girls. Still, you could have settled down with that surly friend of yours and looked after his father's sheep."

"It's the age." It was hard to speak of feelings that seemed to slip away before I could express them. "I was wondering during my watch last night if Fate did not set a seal upon every generation so that whether we are born in Wales, Ireland or Brittany the same questions plague us."

"That is no answer to my question. Why have you followed me here?"

What reply could I give? To find out what had happened to Gawain after he sailed from Belerion? Alas, that would be mere foolishness. To look for truth? Friedowald would laugh. "Tell me something first," I said in an effort to gain time, "have you already landed on this island?"

"I am not as fanciful as you are, Ruan, I only value facts. Five summers ago, while you were still in Cornwall, a wind blew the ship that I was on further and further to the west. The seas went down but we found ourselves in a fog. We drifted for days, seeing neither sun nor stars but it was luckily not cold enough for ice. I think most of us had given up hope that we should ever see our homes again when the mist lifted suddenly, our captain shouted 'Land!' and to our surprise we anchored safely in a sandy bay under some low hills. We rowed ashore to dry our clothes and fill the casks up with some of the sweetest water that we had ever tasted."

"Was there a village?"

"No, we climbed a hill but saw no smoke nor any sign of settlement, yet the soil was rich, I turned it over with a haft and the moors were full of berries that were not fully ripe. I would have gone further but the captain was anxious. He wanted to sail before the fog came down again but the weather was fair and I noted our position as we were sailing back. We shall not go hungry, Ruan, the cattle will prosper and there is enough land for us all."

I had not thought until this moment that this might be the last of all my voyages. "Suppose some of us get homesick?" I asked, gripping a spar as the *Walrus* gave a sudden roll.

"I told you to stay behind with Melvas," Friedowald growled, "if you are longing for your friends already, why did you come?"

"I shall not ask you for oxen but a boat. Not to go back but to go forward. There must be other islands in the ocean besides yours."

"Now I believe you, Ruan, you really heard the singing because, once the surge gets into a man's ears, he will wander for the rest of his life. Help me to build my hall and wait till the cows have increased a little and then I will give you the *Walrus,* that is, if she survives the winter gales. I do not want to draw raiders upon my land but neither you nor your comrades know enough to find me once the winds have blown you east again. You can have the ship but I shall not give you my chart."

"Most of the crew will stay with you," I said. More than half had lost their families in some coastal attack or were discontented with the changes that were creeping across the West. "We shall have to sail because there will not be enough of us to row."

Easterly? Why had he used that word? Did Friedowald know what I still had not confessed to myself: that if I returned it would be to another uncharted island, to Ennis Mor floating on its ancient, silver sea? It was a vague and distant wish, much had to happen first and I was glad that the future seemed as obscure as the fog that had hampered the Finn during his first voyage. "I wondered what happened to Lydd?" I said idly. "Do you suppose the guards were set on him?"

"Lydd!" Friedowald burst into his sea monster laughter again. "Lydd is like groundsel, get it into your fields and you never get it out. He had made himself far too useful to Nera, or so I heard, to be left to Moram's rage. No, all he had to do was to vanish into the forest for a week or two until things were arranged. What a fright he gave you, though! I shall never forget how you ran up to me that day, like a trembling puppy scrambling up a river bank, but it was fortunate, all the same, I got the cows with the gold you gave me so gladly for your passage."

I had to laugh too and the Finn patted me on the shoulder as if he had forgiven me my carelessness. The breeze freshened, there was a sudden lurch, and one of the calves slipped sideways in its pen. It was strange how quickly the animals had learned to steady themselves by pressing against the boards that we had covered with old sacks. A boy brought up a bale of hay from the stores and stroked the soft muzzle with his rough hand. Even the ship seemed to feel that a harbor was in front of her, the timber creaked and the ropes strained as if she were competing in some race.

Our sailmaker was staring at the rollers, they spread out like a quiver cut in half with darts tumbling, rainbow fashion, from the crest of one breaker to the next. We could hear the cook scouring his cauldron before he began the evening meal. "The waves are shortening," Friedowald said, "we shall light the Midsummer beacons on our own shore." My guilt had lifted; I knew at last that the course that had been right for Honorius would have destroyed me as it had harmed Lydd. My way was with the wanderers. We were the sea's children and, if our voyages seemed to cross and circle without apparent purpose, we should understand the pattern in good time. Life existed only as it developed through experience. I could still hear a faint "Ask" surging through my ears but this time without impatience as if the question itself were its own reply.

Friedowald appeared to have gone happily to sleep. I yawned myself and my nostrils seemed to fill with the scent of blackberries and crushed bracken while I followed a path in sunlight to a place where there were neither enemies nor fear. I was dreaming perhaps but I had left everything that I had ever known behind me and as my comrades came forward to relieve the watch the design seemed to draw itself into a fleeting instant of perfection and I went forward thankfully to take my turn at the lookout.